DADDY'S CLIMBING TREE

Also by C. S. Adler

Always and Forever Friends
Carly's Buck
The Cat That Was Left Behind
Ghost Brother
The Lump in the Middle
Tuna Fish Thanksgiving

DADDY'S CLIMBING TREE

By C.S. Adler

CLARION BOOKS / New York

With thanks to my dear friend Miki Boehm for her wise critical
eye and her help with literary problem solving.

Clarion Books
a Houghton Mifflin Company imprint
215 South Park Avenue South, New York, NY 10003
Text copyright © 1993 by Carole S. Adler

Library of Congress Cataloging-in-Publication Data

Adler, C. S. (Carole S.)
Daddy's climbing tree / by C.S. Adler.
p. cm.
Summary: Eleven-year-old Jessica refuses to believe the reality of her father's
death when he is killed in a hit-and-run accident.
ISBN 0-395-63032- 0
[1. Death—Fiction. 2. Fathers and daughters—Fiction.]
I. Title.
PZ7.A26145Dad 1993
[Fic]—dc20   92-6073
                                                                   CIP
                                                                    AC

BP 10 9 8 7 6 5 4 3 2

For Lauren Beth Adler,
*What her dad would wish for her —
a life full of love and achievement.*

DADDY'S CLIMBING TREE

Chapter One

The late June evening started out in such an ordinary way that it made what happened all the harder to believe.

Jessica felt the warm weight of her father's arms on her shoulders and his chin resting on her head as she sat at the kitchen table. She was helping her six-year-old brother, Tycho, make a sign for his bedroom door.

"Come for a run with me, Jessie baby. I'm going to get us some ice cream," Dad said from the top of her head.

She rubbed her cheek against the springy blond hairs on his thick arm. "It's raining out, Daddy."

"A little rain won't melt us."

"Jessica's helping me," Tycho protested.

"And ice cream isn't going to help *you* lose weight, Robbie," Mom called from the bare dining room. She was sitting cross-legged on the floor studying books of wallpaper samples. She hadn't had a dining room in their house in Oldminesville where Daddy had been raised, and where Jessica had lived her whole life — until last week when they'd moved here to Hammond.

"I was planning to buy frozen yogurt," Daddy said. His deep voice hummed with injured virtue.

"I'll bet!" Mom said. "With nuts and chocolate chunks."

"Listen, skinny woman —" Dad called Mom that when he wanted to get back at her for nagging him about his weight. "I'll bet I'm not the only one eating this ice cream."

"Yogurt, you said," Mom reminded him.

"Never mind. If none of my beloved family will brave the elements with me for a little four-mile run, I'll just have to run alone." Dad lifted himself from Jessica's back and shambled to the kitchen door. There he paused and wheedled, "Last chance, Jessie baby."

He looked so silly in his neon pink running shorts and shapeless tee shirt printed with the name of his hospital's softball team that Jessica was tempted. She'd always gone on errands with her big, blond, teddy bear father for the pleasure of having him to herself, but tonight she ached from rearranging her bedroom. She had needed to make it look different from her room in Oldminesville because it hurt too much to wake each morning to the sorry echo of the house she had lost.

Regretfully, she shook her head. "I can't, Daddy. You hurry back."

"Be home in an hour," he said and left.

Tycho raised his freckled, snub-nosed face from his task to ask Jessica, "What else should I put on the sign?" So far it said simply, "Tycho's room."

"I don't know," Jessica said. "What do you want to say? 'Keep out, this means you. Danger zone. Private.' I don't know."

"Well, what are you going to say on your sign?" Tycho's blue eyes took her seriously. Daddy teased, Mom sniped, but Tycho respected her.

"Just, 'Kittens welcome; people please knock.' "

"But you don't have a kitten anymore."

Jessica flinched. Only a couple of weeks had passed since Mimsy was accidentally killed by the tractor in Oldminesville.

"I said she could get another cat, Tycho," Mom commented from the dining room.

"Then can I have a dog?" he was quick to ask.

"Not till you're old enough to take care of it."

"I'm old enough," Tycho said. "Because I'm old enough to be in my own room, aren't I?" Not for nothing had he been named after the long-ago mathematical genius whom Dad admired.

"Let's see how you take care of your room first," Mom said. She was spreading out a bold, blue-flowered pattern against the wall. "Jessica, what do you think of this one? Do you think it's too wild?"

"Yes," Jessica said.

It was Mom's fault they had left Oldminesville. She

had said the commute to her teaching job in Hammond was too long, and the old house had too many problems. She wanted a shiny white kitchen with all new appliances and a garage attached to the house. Fine, so Mom had what she wanted now, but she couldn't make Jessica be happy here by bribing her with a new kitten. And not by asking her opinion about the wallpaper either.

"I like old things best," Jessica had told Mom more than once. How could Mom think any cat could ever replace cuddly Mimsy or any house ever be as dear as the grandparents' Victorian farmhouse? Daddy loved it, too. He had inherited it along with the apple orchard and his climbing tree and the masses of lilac bushes that perfumed the air in May.

"Well, I *like* this pattern," Mom said. Her face, which was as cute and snub-nosed as Tycho's, looked fierce as her eyes narrowed with determination.

An hour later she plopped down beside Jessica and Tycho on the living-room couch. They were channel hopping with the remote button to find something funny on TV. Mom curled her slender legs in their tights and soft leather slippers up under her and said, "I wonder what's keeping your father."

"Oh, you know Daddy. He's probably yakking with somebody or getting a car out of a ditch again," Jessica said.

"Probably," Mom agreed, but she hopped up fast to answer the phone when it rang.

Next thing Jessica knew Mom was standing in the doorway, blank faced. In a hollow voice, she said, "I have to go to the hospital. Your father got hurt."

"He did? What happened?" Jessica asked.

"I don't know. They said a car skidded. I don't know, Jessica. I'll call you when I find out how he is." She clutched her purse. "Meanwhile, you take care of Tycho for me, okay?" She left without waiting for Jessica's reply.

Even when she was small, Jessica had never been confused about what was real and what wasn't. She had always known that a monster under the bed was make-believe, and the one on TV who took hostages and started wars was real. Make-believe was when she played teacher with her little brother. Real was taking the matches away from him when Mom and Daddy weren't around.

Now she was eleven. She was the big sister. And so she was quite certain that it wasn't real when three television programs later Mom came back from the hospital and said, "Children, I don't know how to say this. Come here to me now." She held out her arms, and when she had encircled Jessica and Tycho, she said breathlessly, "What happened was the road was wet and the car skidded, and your father — Robbie was running, and the car hit him. They say he didn't suffer. He just —" Her voice went up high. "Your father's dead," she said.

Mom didn't sound like herself. Her eyes staring at them from dark sockets seemed distant as a stranger's. "No, he's not," Jessica said. She pulled away from her mother.

"Did Daddy get the ice cream — I mean, the frozen yogurt?" Tycho asked.

Mom made a funny sound in her nose.

Alan walked in then. Jessica looked at him hopefully. Shy, quiet Alan had been Daddy's college roommate, and he belonged to their family. At least, Jessica felt he did because he shared so many of their fun times, and he helped Daddy with chores and ran errands for Mom. Before Jessica had turned eleven, he'd often babysat for her and Tycho.

"I put your car in the garage," Alan said to Mom. "I'll take a cab back to pick up mine at the hospital."

"They don't believe me, Alan," Mom said.

"I don't believe it either yet," Alan told her. His narrow face squeezed together painfully above his soft brown beard. "I can't figure how it could happen. . . . Unless his glasses fogged up so he couldn't see. Robbie's glasses were always fogging up in the rain."

Mom shook her head. She said, "The sheriff told me it wasn't anybody's fault. It was just an accident. . . . They asked if I wanted his running shoes. As if anyone could wear Robbie's sneakers! His feet are so big he had to special order them from a king-size catalog." She let out a wail and tears streamed down her cheeks.

Mom was acting really crazy.

Jessica turned to ask Alan, who stood there with his hands stretched out helplessly, "Do you know where Daddy is?"

"I don't know anything," Alan said. "Your mother called and asked me to drive her home from the hospital, but I didn't see him." As his eyes met Jessica's, he licked his lips as if he were going to say something more, but then he didn't. Alan never said much. Jessica thought that might be why he was a bachelor and had so few friends.

Mom was still crying. Her fingers pulled out tissues from the pockets of the loose blue-striped shirt she was wearing over her workout tights. Her long black hair was a snarly mess, which was strange because Mom always took care to look perfect even on weekends. Jessica was the one who let her blond hair fly and wore comfortable old clothes.

An arm snaked through Jessica's. "Daddy couldn't get killed, could he?" Tycho whispered in her ear.

"No," Jessica said. "Of course not. Come on, Tycho. It's past your bedtime."

"I don't want to go to bed."

"Don't you want me to read you the chapter about the Emerald City?" she coaxed him. Daddy had given her *The Wizard of Oz* when she was two. She loved reading it to Tycho because the illustrations were so beautiful and because she still enjoyed becoming Dorothy.

"Okay," Tycho agreed.

He went to kiss his mother good night, but she clutched him and collapsed onto the couch sobbing, "My baby!"

Tycho wriggled free, looking scared. When he *was* a baby Mom used to say that Tycho thought Jessica was his mother because she spent so much time with him. "Think we ought to keep him?" Mom had asked her slyly, because Jessica had suggested they send Tycho back to the hospital when she first saw him and he was so tiny and demanding.

Now Mom's strangely contorted face alarmed Jessica who said scornfully, "If anybody's interested, it's way past Tycho's bedtime." Then she grabbed Tycho by the hand and marched him up the six steps to the bedroom landing.

"We'll get you ice cream tomorrow, Tycho," she said in a soothing big-sister voice. Over her shoulder, she glimpsed Mom in a crumpled heap in Alan's arms. He was patting her back and looking around vaguely as if he were wishing Daddy would walk in and take over. Jessica compressed her lips and told Tycho to hurry up and get in his pajamas and she'd meet him in the bathroom. He needed someone to supervise the way he brushed his teeth or he'd just stand there chewing on the toothbrush and spitting in the sink.

He had on his turtle pajamas when he joined her in the bathroom. Jessica handed him the toothbrush with the right amount of paste on it and watched to make sure he brushed inside and topside and outside as well.

Tycho stood on the scale beside the washbowl and leaned against the towels. He looked funny tucked under the towel rack like that. As her friend Jia Jia said, Jessica was lucky that Tycho was so cute and not a brat like their friend Jenny's little brother.

"But what happened to Daddy, Jessica?" Tycho asked through toothpaste-coated teeth.

"I don't know. Maybe he's playing a trick on us. You know how he likes to fool around."

"But Mom said a car hit him."

"That's stupid," Jessica said. "Daddy's too big to get hit by a car. You think he's a little kid, like you? Hurry up, and wash your face and hands now." Jessica even rinsed the toothbrush for him.

She said she'd get the book. But she felt ill — hot and cold, as if she had a fever — so instead of getting the book, she leaned her head against the cool, rain-washed window in her lemon-colored bedroom. The room didn't wrap itself around her the way her old room had. It didn't comfort her at all. In fact, it felt unreal. Like this business about Daddy being hit by a car. That was unreal, too — something that couldn't happen. Mimsy could get killed, yes, and they could move away from Oldminesville, yes, but nothing could happen to Daddy. He was too necessary, too essential, like sunlight was, or air or food.

He couldn't suddenly be gone as if he didn't matter. He just couldn't.

Chapter Two

Rain glinted in the light from the street lamp. It made silvery streaks on the black asphalt road and on the car parked in the driveway across the street. In Oldminesville only a soft dirt road was visible between the grandparents' house and the highway. Nobody else's house was in sight there, just the barn and the woods, and past the field the broad arms of Daddy's climbing tree.

How strange it was that here there should be a mirror image of their split-level across the street, except no girl like Jessica looked back from it. Mom had said there'd be lots of girls her age in all these look-alike houses in the development. "You won't lose your friends Jia Jia and Jenny; you'll just add new friends," Mom had said.

That was another lie, like Mom's claim that Jessica would be happy in Hammond where the library was bigger and shopping was more convenient. As if Mom didn't know that Jessica needed to live where there were woods and space for trees to open their arms wide to the sky! What Jessica resented most was that no matter how she tried to tell her, Mom didn't hear. She would only hear what suited her, whatever agreed with what Mom wanted for herself.

A cat slipped under the parked car to take shelter from the rain. Jessica's heart clutched painfully even though this was a black cat, not gray and white like Mimsy had been. What would make her feel better was to see Daddy's solid arms and legs pumping up the road as he ran home to them. His broad face would be smiling, and his eyes behind his glasses would be making blue-eyed sunshine in the rain. "Mom," Jessica would call to her mother, "Mom, I told you he'd be back."

"I'm waiting for you, Jessica." Tycho's voice startled her. She turned and saw him standing barefooted in her doorway. "Didn't you find the book?"

"I'm getting it," she said. She picked it off the floor where she'd ranged her books along three walls, using furniture as bookends. The bookshelf was filled with stuffed animals, dressed in the hats and collars and vests that she'd made for them.

"Jessica . . ." Mom said. She had suddenly appeared behind Tycho in the doorway. Her eyes were reddened and she still hadn't combed her hair, but she looked more normal. "I came up to see how you're doing. Are you —?"

"I'm fine. I'm going to read to Tycho."

Mom bent to give Tycho another hug.

"Is Daddy home yet?" Tycho asked.

"Oh, Tycho!" Mom said in a jagged voice. "I told you, darling. He's not coming home. Daddy's gone. He got killed."

"No, he didn't," Tycho said. His eyes went to his sister to confirm what she had told him.

"When can I see him?" Jessica asked her mother coolly.

"Your father? . . . Oh, you mean his body? I don't know, honey. I'll have to call the funeral parlor and ask. But are you sure you really want to?" She paused. "Although, since he wanted to be cremated, there won't be any body at the funeral, so I suppose —"

"CREMATED? BURNED UP?" Jessica screamed. "Now I know you're lying. You wouldn't do that to Daddy."

Mom looked startled. "Well," she said unhappily, "he told me that's what he wanted if — He said he'd want his ashes scattered on some mountain trail we've hiked. Of course, he didn't expect to die. He just said it. But I remember because it was our last anniversary." Mom put her hand over her mouth. She sounded as if she were strangling.

Jessica shook her head. "Liar," she said. "You're a liar, Mom."

Tycho caught his breath and stared at Jessica, who had never spoken that way to her mother before.

Mom quieted. "Jessica, why are you so mad at me? I

didn't hurt him. You know that. I love him as much as you do."

Stubbornly, Jessica bent her head to *The Wizard of Oz* and began turning pages. She had asked when she could see Daddy to trick Mom into saying where he was. How could Mom think it was a body Jessica wanted to see? And then for Mom to talk about cremation, as if anything so awful could have to do with Daddy!

"You don't believe it happened, do you?" Mom said. "I suppose it is hard when it was so sudden. Maybe I'd better call and ask them if you and Tycho can see him before they — before the funeral." She held out her arms to Jessica, but Jessica stepped into the narrow space between the bed and the window where she couldn't be reached. She was tall and big-boned like her father. For a long time she had felt awkward being embraced by her slip of a mother.

"It's just us now, Jessica," Mom said. "Please, darling. We have to do what we can to help each other."

Liar, Jessica accused her mother silently. Liar, liar, liar. It was Daddy whom Jessica was close to, Daddy who always understood her, Daddy who came home from his job as a nurse in the recovery room at the hospital eager to be with her.

When Mom got home from teaching, she either wanted to lie down and take a nap or get on the telephone and talk. Lately it was about the new contract the teachers were negotiating in Hammond. Mom was always on some committee about improving the curriculum or communications with the community or a new contract. She spent a lot of her time at home organizing things outside it, Jessica thought, and not much time at all being with her children.

"Aren't we going to get any ice cream?" Tycho asked Mom. He was clinging to her. She had taken him into her arms when Jessica backed off.

"Not tonight, angel," Mom said. "Come on; I'll put you to bed."

Jessica stood waiting while Mom took Tycho to his room. She was still standing and waiting when Mom stopped in her doorway to say, "He wants you, Jessica."

"Okay."

"You do understand, don't you, darling?"

"Yes," Jessica said to get rid of her.

"Do you want to talk about it?"

"No. . . . I have to read to Tycho now."

Mom hesitated. Then she said, "If you need me, I'll be in the kitchen. I have to call his family and all our friends." Her footsteps tapped a sad message down the staircase.

When she was sure her mother was gone, Jessica went to Tycho's room.

"Why are you so mean to Mommy?" he asked her.

"She's the one who's mean," Jessica said. She settled on the bed on the side near the lighted circus lamp, opened the book, and began to read. Tycho was clutching Bucky Baby, the stuffed rabbit Jessica had given him that was now threadbare and whiskerless. He had stopped sucking his thumb last year when he started kindergarten because he didn't want kids to think he was a baby. But as she began reading, he turned away from her and tucked his thumb in his mouth.

"It's okay, Tycho," Jessica said, keeping her finger on the place where she'd stopped reading. "It's a mistake. Daddy's coming back."

He pulled his thumb out of his mouth to say, "But Mom said —"

"Mom doesn't know everything," Jessica told him confidently. "Do you want me to read to you or not?"

"Read," he said, and he snuggled against her the way he used to when he'd crept into her bed in the room they shared in Oldminesville. She liked it when he snuggled. Next to Daddy, she loved Tycho best.

Jessica read mechanically. She was wondering if her friend Jia Jia would get someone to bring her over tomorrow. Jia Jia and she had been best friends since first grade, when Jia Jia had moved to Oldminesville from Taiwan. Her name meant "good" in Chinese. Jessica and Jia Jia, they were the Jays, just the two of them before Jenny had come to their school last year.

Only last week Jia Jia and she had seen the nuthatches leave their nest in the yard of the parsonage, where Jia Jia's father was a minister. They hadn't told Jenny about the baby nuthatches. She wouldn't have had the patience to sit quietly and watch hour after hour, day after day, to see the parents flying in endless deliveries of food. It wouldn't have interested Jenny to wonder how many babies they were feeding, and if they'd all live, and whether any would fall to the ground or if they'd fly right away.

When the five nuthatch babies had launched themselves one after the other, each in its own direction, Jessica had been thrilled. She hadn't needed to say anything to Jia Jia to know she was, too. They didn't need words to know each other's feelings.

"Then why's Mom crying, Jessica?" Tycho interrupted her reading to ask.

"Because. Don't worry. Daddy wouldn't die on us, believe me."

"But Mom said —"

"She's lying. Or he's fooling her. Anyway, he's alive."

"But where is he?"

"He's waiting for us to find him."

"So when are we going to look?"

"Pretty soon. . . . I promise. . . . Did I ever lie to you?"

He didn't have to think before saying, "Yes, you did."

"When?"

"About the stickers."

"Oh," she said and stopped to consider. True, she had lied to him about his animal stickers. When she needed to use some of them to decorate the cover of her report, he hadn't been around to ask, so she'd just taken them.

Later, he'd noticed they were gone, and she'd been embarrassed because she'd done what she told him never to do. She had said she didn't know what had happened to his stickers, and she had hidden her report. Except then she had brought her report home with an A on it, and he had recognized his stickers and said, "That wasn't nice, Jessica. You didn't ask me."

"Well, I knew you'd give them to me anyway."

"But you took them without asking, and you said never do that."

"Oh, poop. So what?"

"So then you lied."

She hadn't talked to him for a whole evening — she'd been that angry, as much at herself as at him. He'd made her feel so rotten.

"Anyway," she told Tycho as she turned a page of *The Wizard of Oz,* "I'm not lying now. We'll find Daddy, you'll see."

"Good." Tycho sighed. "I don't want him to be dead."

"Well, he *isn't,*" Jessica said with passion.

Chapter Three

An icy sliver of fear cut through Jessica's dreaming and awakened her. Immediately she hurried to her parents' bedroom to check that her father was there. He wasn't, but she calmed herself. Dad was up and out already, sipping his mug of coffee while he watched the mist rise. Or he was down in the kitchen making waffles because it was Saturday and he always made something special on Saturdays.

Jessica stopped by Tycho's door. He was still asleep, cheek to cheek with his washed-out Bucky Baby in a room bright with morning sunshine. Well, he'd been up late last night. Downstairs, Mom was on the kitchen phone. She sounded impatient, the way she did when someone was being hard to convince.

"Of course, Michelle," Mom was saying. "Of course I know how it is with an eight-week-old baby. But he was your brother and even if it is a long drive — he was your *brother* and he'd want you to be here."

Jessica focused on the part about the baby. It would be nice if Aunt Michelle brought the baby. It was a girl and Jessica had made her a pink fabric ball embroidered with the alphabet, but she'd never seen her new cousin. Before Tycho was born, Jessica had hoped for a sister. Even now when he got into a wild mood and jumped around pretending to be a cartoon character he'd seen on television, she still wished he'd been a girl.

She trailed into the kitchen in the old tee shirt of her father's that she slept in. It disappointed her not to find Daddy cooking something. But no wonder. It was already nine according to the clock on the oven. Daddy was probably working out in the yard or off on an errand.

Mom hung up the phone. "Honestly, that family!" she said to Jessica. "When you think of all your father's done for them — You better get some clothes on quick-in-a-hurry, Jessica. People will be dropping by all day. . . . Honey? How are you feeling? Did you sleep all right?"

"Uh huh."

"Well, come give me a hug. You look as if you need one." The phone rang, and Mom snatched it off the cradle.

"Breakfast, breakfast, breakfast," Jessica reminded herself. She opened the refrigerator and stared at the juice container.

". . . He went out to get us some ice cream. Running in that rain, yes, but —"

Not hearing things was easy. In school, Jessica often got so absorbed in her own thoughts that she didn't hear the teachers. Daydreaming, they called it, but since she usually managed to come up with the right answer, they didn't get angry at her. The juice container reminded her of the camping trip last summer when Tycho had used a similar jar for the fishing worms, and Daddy had made the powdered orange juice on top of them without looking. He had strained out the worms and drunk the juice anyway, but none of the rest of them would.

"Can I have one, too?" Tycho asked, there beside her suddenly.

Momentarily bewildered, Jessica turned from her brother's pajama-clad figure to the toaster where an English muffin was cooking. Had she put it there? Probably. "Sure," she said. She even gave Tycho half of her toasted muffin instead of making him wait for his own.

"He's being cremated," Mom said on the phone to someone. "Well, it's what he wanted. Yes, there'll be a service — in the funeral parlor tomorrow. . . . Yes, I know it's a six-hour drive for you from Pennsylvania, Brad, and — But most people can get here by then, and he's your *brother* and Sunday afternoon's as late as —"

Tycho was playing with his half muffin, worrying it with a finger instead of eating it warm.

"Do you want to eat your muffin in front of the TV and watch your cartoons?" Jessica asked him.

"I don't feel like watching cartoons."

"So don't."

"You said we were going to find Daddy."

"We will. I just have to figure out where he is."

"Well, why does Mom have all these people coming?"

"How should I know? Because that's the way she is." Jessica folded her lips in and commanded, "Eat your muffin."

"You didn't butter it for me."

"Tycho, don't be such a baby. You can butter your own muffin."

"But you do it better."

"Children, don't fuss, not this morning!" Mom said. The phone was back on the hook. "Let's be extra nice to each other today. I know you're hurting and it's hard, but we have to try and get through this."

Mom ran her fingers through her long hair. She had on the same clothes she'd worn yesterday. Mom almost never wore the same clothes twice, and her face looked so puffy and ill that she wasn't even pretty. Jessica shivered with foreboding.

The phone rang again. Mom picked it up automatically. "Oh, Annie, I kept trying to reach you last night. How'd you find out? . . . What? . . . You don't know? Oh, Annie, Robbie — last night, Robbie went out for ice cream and —"

"Come on, Tycho," Jessica said loudly. "I'm going to get dressed and you can eat pretzels while you watch your cartoons."

"Mom won't let me." Tycho loved pretzels, the big hard crunchy kind with salt crystals that Daddy bought and Mom said were bad for them.

"Today you can have them. Mom won't care." Jessica crackled the pretzel bag noisily to drown out her mother's voice on the phone.

Annie was Mom's oldest friend. Would she come, too, all the way from Burlington, Vermont? It had taken half a day when they drove to visit her last August. Annie was also a teacher, but she didn't have any children. She'd been a foster child like Mom. In fact, they'd met in a foster home. It was not having family of her own that made Mom fuss so much about Dad's family, he'd told Jessica. And he'd said that she should be kind to her mother, that Mom needed a lot of loving. For a minute Jessica felt guilty, but why should she when Mom was so good at taking care of herself?

Back upstairs, Jessica put on her old, faded pink knit pants and a stained pink and lavender knit shirt. She hoped Mom wouldn't make her change into something newer for the guests. Annie wouldn't expect her to look special, but Mom might want Tycho and her to dress up for Dad's relatives.

Alan arrived first. Mom was still on the phone, so he came into the living room where Jessica was watching TV with Tycho. "How are you guys doing?"

"Fine," Tycho said.

Jessica eyed Alan and asked him, "Why are you wearing a tie?"

He squinted at her with that pained look left over from last night, as if he might cry. "I guess I thought I should in honor of your father," he said sadly.

Jessica had no patience with his sadness. "Daddy doesn't care about clothes," she said.

"I know," Alan said. "But a lot of people are coming from school and probably from the hospital."

As if on cue, the doorbell rang. Jessica stayed put, leaving Alan to open the door. It was a neighbor from Oldminesville, the large old lady with blue hair who had given Mimsy to Jessica. She thrust a casserole dish at Alan.

"It's creamed chicken and vegetables. The children need to eat and Judy won't want to cook at a time like this." The woman stepped into the living room and noticed Jessica and Tycho in front of the TV. "How are you doing, you two?" she asked heartily.

"Hi, Mrs. Monroe," Jessica said. To discourage conversation, she stared at the TV as if the stupid cartoon cat on the roller coaster interested her.

"I see you're eating your breakfast in front of the TV. Does your mother usually let you do that?"

"Not usually," Jessica said. Mrs. Monroe was eyeing Tycho's uneaten half muffin and the bag of pretzels.

"I don't expect your poor mother feels much like cooking. I brought a chicken and vegetable casserole that you could heat for supper, Jessica."

"Yes. Thank you." Jessica stared past Mrs. Monroe, willing her to leave. Mrs. Monroe didn't know much if she thought Mom *ever* liked cooking. It was Daddy who liked it. Whenever he was home in time, he cooked dinner. He liked noodle things with cheese or with fresh tomatoes cut up in them and sauteed green peppers. He liked stir-fried dishes too, and he made them taste delicious.

What Mom did was the cleanup. Since she worked so fast that it was hard to help her, Jessica's only job was to set the table. Most of the time Mom had to remind her to do even that. What Jessica liked was making a flower arrangement for the table, like daisies and irises in the blue pot, or a fat bowl filled with the white roses that still grew by the barn in Oldminesville.

Mom came to greet Mrs. Monroe just as the phone rang again. "Could someone get that, please?" Mom asked. The doorbell chimed. Alan went to the door. Nobody answered the telephone. Three rings and the answering machine came on.

"Hi, we're glad you called, but Judy and I can't come to the phone right now," Dad's deep voice crooned on the machine. "How about leaving us a message and we'll get back to you." Hearing her father's voice mesmerized Jessica so that she didn't even hear Alan calling her to the door.

"Jessica, it's us," Jenny shrieked.

That Jessica heard. She stood up and saw Jenny with her pink-cheeked mother. Beside Jenny's mother stood Jia Jia. Her narrow dark eyes shone with all the wordless understanding Jessica craved.

24

"Jessica," Jenny's mother said. "Jessica, I'm so sorry." Her high, sweet, chatty voice was strained. "The only way I could think to help you was to bring your friends over. Or would you rather wait to see them some other time? After the funeral when you're ready for company?"

Jessica stared at the four pearly white buttons on Jenny's mother's blouse to avoid the drenching sympathy on her face. It was like the time Jessica had scraped her arm and Jenny's mother made such a sickening fuss with antiseptic and bandages. Without exactly answering her question, Jessica said, "Hi, Jenny. Hi, Jia Jia. Want to come upstairs and see my new bedroom? We could play up there."

Jia Jia didn't move. Quietly, she said, "I'm very sorry about your father." Then her lips turned up in a smile and she flipped her seal-black hair over her shoulder and added, "I'd like to play Scattergories."

"Or we could play music and dance," Jenny suggested. Her mother shoved her from behind. "I'm very sorry —" Jenny began awkwardly.

"Let's go upstairs," Jessica interrupted her. She raced up the six steps to the bedroom landing, then happened to glance back at the couch. Tycho was still there, clutching a pillow to his chest, his thumb suspended midway to his mouth. "You can come, too, Tycho," she said.

He beamed and bounded across the room after her.

Closing her bedroom door firmly against all the doorbell and phone ringing, Jessica said happily, "Let's play Scattergories first."

"It's different," Jia Jia said about the way Jessica had arranged the room. "Sort of funny with the bears in the bookcase and the books on the floor. I like it."

"Thanks," Jessica said.

"It's bigger than your old bedroom," Jenny added, "and much brighter."

"No, it isn't," Jessica said coldly.

Two hours later Jenny said meaningfully to Jessica, "I'm sort of thirsty." She never minded asking for things. After she came to their school last year and pointed out that she was a Jay, too, Jessica had asked Jia Jia if she liked Jenny.

"I like the way she bubbles," Jia Jia had said. "And she always has something to say." Since Jia Jia liked her, Jessica had to, also. Only now that she'd moved, she hoped Jia Jia didn't forget who her true best friend was.

Jessica took her friends to the refrigerator. Mom was at the sink being hugged by two teachers from her school. The kitchen table was jammed with containers of food and fruit trays, and Alan was lugging in a basket of flowers so big it hid his whole head. It seemed as if they were in the midst of a huge party.

"And how are you doing, young lady?" It was the toothy heart specialist who had told Mom that her husband's sympathy cured patients better than any drug. "Robbie's an amazingly loving man," she had said.

"I'm doing fine," Jessica said. Before the doctor could

ask her anything else, she spun on her heel toward her mother and asked, "Mom, can we have juice or soda or something?"

"Anything you can find in the fridge, honey." Mom's face was still puffy and tears were running down her cheeks. Where did they all come from? Jessica wondered as she opened the refrigerator door.

She felt safer when the heart doctor gave up on her and walked over to talk to Alan.

"Want a cream cheese, nut, and raisin sandwich?" Jessica asked her friends.

"My favorite," Jia Jia said, but Jenny wanted peanut butter. Tycho said he'd have peanut butter with mayonnaise.

"Ew, yecch!" Jenny said. "Who could eat a combination like that?"

"Tycho likes it," Jia Jia said loyally, and she made him his sandwich while Jessica did the others. Jenny watched Tycho take his first bite as if he were a circus act. He was the only one who'd been able to squeeze out a place on the kitchen table for his lunch.

"Let's eat outside," Jessica suggested. Eager to escape the emotional traps indoors, she led her friends to the redwood picnic table from Oldminesville. It had been abandoned on the bare, grass-covered area behind the house.

"Look," Jenny said, pointing to the table. "Here's where we carved our names." It had been her idea, but Jia Jia had made the fancy lettering. Jia Jia and Jessica

27

sat side by side, eating their sandwiches in silence while Jenny chattered about some flavored lipstick her mother had let her buy. Competing with her for their attention were a music station on somebody's radio and a growling lawn mower.

Quietly, Jessica said to her friends, "I'm glad you finally got here. I've missed you so much."

"Maybe your mother will move back to Oldminesville now," Jenny said.

"What do you mean?" Jessica turned on her abruptly. "Why should she? She likes it here." She looked down the alley of lawns that stretched behind the naked backs of the development houses. There were several swing sets, but only one tree swayed its branches to the wind.

"It's a really long drive," Jia Jia said, "It took us nearly an hour because you have to drive all the way around the state park."

"Well, you can stay over when you come to visit," Jessica said.

"I'd come," Jenny said, "but we're leaving for Minnesota next week to visit my grandparents."

Jessica bit her lip and asked, "Are you going to do computers at the arts and science camp again this summer, Jia Jia?"

Jia Jia nodded.

"Anyway, we still have weekends," Jessica said.

"And *you* can visit *me*," Jia Jia said. "If your mother will drive."

"Have you made any friends yet?" Jenny asked.

"She's only been here a week," Jia Jia answered for her.

"What you should do, Jessica," Jenny instructed her, "is hang out at the library and the pool and talk to people — just anybody who comes along. That's how I'd make friends here this summer."

Jia Jia laughed. "Jessica goes to the library to find books and to the pool to swim. She's not a talker like you, Jenny."

"What I like best about summer," Jessica said dreamily, "is being able to do what I want. I mean slow things like —"

"Watching flowers grow," Jia Jia teased. "Chasing butterflies."

Jessica laughed.

"And sleeping late," Jenny said.

"Yes," Jessica said. "And we'll go camping. Daddy always —" She stopped and swallowed.

"When will you get another kitten?" Jia Jia asked quickly.

"Oh, are you getting a new kitten, Jessica? You're so lucky," Jenny said. "I mean you would be if —"

Jessica shrugged. Something big and heavy had settled in her chest and she felt dizzy suddenly.

"Let's walk around your neighborhood and see what other kids are doing," Jia Jia suggested.

"Okay," Jessica said. She went to tell her mother

where she was going and found her talking to the heart specialist. Dr. Miner, that was her name, Jessica remembered.

Mom nodded when Jessica told her about the walk. "Fine, honey. But don't stay away too long."

Tycho was busy with Alan, shooting marbles at a plastic top, so there wasn't any need to invite her brother to come with them.

She was glad to swing arms with her friends as they explored the look-alike streets of dittoed houses.

"It's nice here," Jenny said. "I like Hammond."

Jia Jia rolled her eyes at the comment. Jessica ignored it.

It was late afternoon when Jenny's mother returned for the girls. "Would you like me to bring them to the service tomorrow, Jessica, so that you have someone your own age to be with you?"

"No, don't do that, please," Jessica said, stiffening herself against the gentle hand rubbing her back and against the next thing that Jenny's mother might say. But then it wasn't Jenny's mother she had to be on guard against after all.

Just as they were getting in the car, Jenny turned around and ran back to the steps, where Jessica was politely watching them go. Throwing her arms around Jessica, Jenny said. "Gee, it's awful about your father. He was the nicest man, Jessica. I'm really, really sorry."

Jessica squeezed her eyes shut and shuddered.

"What's wrong?" Jenny asked in alarm.

"Nothing. Go home, Jenny." Jessica pushed her away and dashed into the house. Dodging through the people sitting everywhere, even on the stairs, she made it to her own bedroom. But there were two ladies sitting on her bed talking. She slipped into Tycho's room. He was alone playing with his race-car track.

"You said you were going to take me to Daddy," he said.

"We'll go. I promised you, didn't I?" Jessica said.

Through his window, she saw another car drive up. Three adults got out. She didn't recognize them. But then she wasn't recognizing anything well anymore. Even the furniture seemed alien. Even she herself. She felt as if she were hidden inside a shape that people recognized as her, but that wasn't. And Mom was acting so weird! Only Tycho was still himself. Except that he looked so sad it hurt to watch him.

Chapter Four

"Jessica, you have to get up now. I know you had a bad night, but if I let you sleep in, we won't have a chance to talk."

Her mother's voice seemed to come from far away until Jessica opened her eyes. There was Mom sitting right beside her on the bed wearing makeup and a dress as if she were going to teach. But school was over.

"What time is it?" Jessica asked.

"It's past ten. People may start arriving any minute. I laid out the dress I bought you that you said is too fancy." Mom's voice was pleading. "You'll wear it for Daddy, won't you?"

Jessica sat up straight. "Is he here?"

"Oh, Jessica!" Mom brushed back the hair plastered to Jessica's cheek. "You know what I mean. For the service. I spoke to the funeral director about what you said you wanted, but he said since there wasn't going to be a coffin, he'd already — And it's better for you to remember your father alive, isn't it? Jessica, are you listening to me?"

"Yes. It's okay. I'll wear the dress."

The window was glazed with sunshine, and a warm breeze tickled Jessica's bare toes. Somebody outside was whistling and calling, "Brandy. Here, Brandy. Come!" But the cheerfulness of the day didn't touch the heavy stone in Jessica's chest.

"Tycho woke me up," she said, remembering how he had screamed in his nightmare. And when she couldn't calm him down, she had gone to get Mom, who wouldn't wake up. That had frightened her so much that she had started screaming, too.

"I took a sleeping pill," Mom said. "That's why you couldn't wake me last night. . . . Jessica, talk to me." Mom took her hands as if to trap her into confiding. "Tell me what you're thinking. It's bad to keep it all inside." Tears promptly slid down Mom's cheeks, endangering her makeup.

"I'm okay," Jessica pulled her hands away and sat up. "But I don't want to go to any service."

"You have to, darling. You'd always regret not going. When we get the ashes in a couple of days, we'll find a mountaintop and have a private ceremony, but this one we have to do for other people so they can say good-bye. So many people loved your father." Mom swallowed hard.

"I can't go today," Jessica said.

"Well, then come because I need you with me. I need your support, Jessica." A new tide of tears flooded Mom's eyes.

While she had been talking, the phone had been ringing. Now the message on the answering machine came on with Dad's voice. Mom pressed her fingers over her lips as she listened. Then she said, "I'd better put another message on right now."

"But I like hearing Daddy's voice," Jessica protested.

"No. . . . No. I can't bear it." Mom hurried out of the room.

Jessica rolled off the bed. Tycho was still asleep across the hall in their parents' king-sized bed, where she'd led him last night when he'd had his nightmare. He was snailed up small in the exact middle. A woman's voice was saying hesitantly on the answering machine, "I'm sorry to bother you, Judy, but we'd like to come to the service, and we don't know the time. The newspaper didn't say."

The doorbell rang. It was going to be a day like yesterday with a house full of people and no peace anywhere. Well, Mom *liked* everything going on at once. Let her handle it. Jessica went to the bathroom. When she was finished, she dutifully put on the soft, flowery cotton dress.

What she disliked about the new dress was that it gave her a fake sweetness like Jenny's mother had, like Jenny had sometimes, especially around adults. It was a disguise, but maybe today being in disguise was a good idea. Jessica yanked the brush through her long, tawny blond hair, for once glad that it hurt.

By the time she was done, Tycho was awake. Mom had set out his good clothes too. "You better get dressed, Tycho. Mom's got more people coming. And you'll see your uncles. They're coming from Pennsylvania."

Tycho's lips drew down in his stubborn turtle look, which meant it would be impossible to hurry him. Jessica didn't even try. She warned him again to get dressed and went downstairs. Alan was talking earnestly with Mom about what car to use and who would drive it.

Jessica tossed him a "hi" and continued on to the kitchen where the fat Sunday paper lay unopened on the table. That voice on the answering machine earlier had mentioned finding something about a service in the paper. Jessica paged through news and ads and special columns until she got to the obituaries.

And there was her father's name.

> Robert Warren Turner, age 34, victim of a hit-and-run accident. Husband of Judith Albert Turner, and father of Jessica and Tycho. Born in Pennsylvania, he was a longtime resident of Oldminesville, and worked as a recovery room nurse for St. Elizabeth's Hospital. A graduate of . . .

Suddenly Jessica's head was spinning and she thought she needed to throw up. She closed the paper and ran to the kitchen sink where rage replaced her nausea. How dare they write about her father like that, as if he weren't here anymore? Any minute now he'd walk in. "What's up, Jessie baby? What are you going to do with all this sunshine?" he'd say, and she'd tell him about the newspaper, and he'd be proud of her that she hadn't lost faith in him. Her daddy would never desert her. That much she knew.

She thought about getting herself some cereal, except she wasn't hungry. Instead, she went out the kitchen door and sat on the back steps. From the doorstep of the house in Oldminesville, she often saw deer browsing in the old apple orchard. Sometimes there were cedar waxwings feasting on berries on the bushes near the house. Daddy and she had listed over twenty-five different kinds of bird visitors to the grandparents' neglected gardens.

But what Jessica longed for most right now was to see the sky half-filled with Daddy's magnificent climbing tree. If she were in Oldminesville, she'd climb the rungs nailed to the trunk to the first outflung branch and spend the morning dreaming out over the valley.

A robin arrived on the sparse lawn to dig for a worm. Once Daddy had tried to tell her that humans and animals had the same goals. "A bug's life is just as important to it as ours is to us. And it's trying to live well, just the way we are," he had said.

"You're silly, Daddy," she had told him. She often called him silly when she didn't understand.

Tycho never did. He just took what he heard and filed it away. Later he might ask about something he didn't quite get. Tycho was smart in his own way. It made Jessica jealous when Daddy taught Tycho things that didn't interest her, like programming the VCR or using a socket wrench. "You like him better than me because he's a boy," she had accused her father.

"How could I like anybody better than you when you're my favorite daughter in this whole world," Daddy would say. He'd sound so sincere that she'd be satisfied, even though the words didn't exactly say what they seemed to say.

"Jessica, there you are," Mom said. "Tycho's taking forever to get dressed, but I see you're ready. And you brushed your hair." Mom smiled and touched Jessica's cheek. "You look lovely, darling. Thanks. Believe me, I know how hard this is for you."

"I hate having people around all the time."

"Well, at least they're a distraction. . . . It would have been easier if this had happened during the school year when there's no time to think. We'll have to keep very busy this summer." Mom's eyes filled with tears again. "Maybe you and I can paint your bedroom together, Jessica. I know you hate that lemon color."

"Daddy's going to paint it with me."

"But he can't now, can he?"

"Mom," Jessica said in sudden panic. "I can't talk to people."

"Just be polite; that's all I expect of you. Which reminds me, we'll have to put up your uncles overnight. I thought I'd put Tycho in your room and give them Tycho's bed."

"Fine."

"Do you mind about not seeing your father's body, Jessica?"

"No."

"Good. It's better to remember him smiling. He had such an amazing smile. I always thought it felt like a warm massage when he smiled at me."

"I don't believe you," Jessica said in a strangled voice.

"About what?" Mom seemed startled.

"About anything," Jessica said bitterly. And before her mother could argue with her, she jumped up. She was meaning to run, except she had no place to run to here that was safe — no climbing tree, no attic or barn or woods. In desperation she ran upstairs to the bathroom and locked herself in.

Tycho banged on the door for a while, then gave up and went away. From the bathroom window, Jessica could see cars pulling into the driveway. She filled the bathtub, defiantly dumped in the rest of Mom's birthday bubble bath, took off her clothes, and got in. Only when her skin began to shrivel did she dry herself and get dressed again.

"You look princess pretty," Daddy would say when he saw her. Of course, she knew she wasn't pretty. Her nose was too long, and except when she smiled, her face was too serious. Mom kept telling her to smile more, but Daddy liked her the way she was.

He was too young to be dead, a lot younger than Jia Jia's father, who was a gray-haired, skinny old man. Besides, they couldn't manage without Dad at the hospital. Hadn't a patient sent him a card just a few days ago that said Daddy was better than a pot of chicken soup and the best healer there? "I think I'll show my boss this and ask for a raise," Daddy had joked.

Downstairs, Jessica found the house full of people again.

A plump young woman grabbed her and said, "Jessica, don't you remember me? I'm your Aunt Michelle."

The last time Jessica had seen Aunt Michelle, she'd been long-haired and thin. Now she was short-haired and potato-shaped, but Jessica smiled at her and allowed herself to be kissed. "Hi," she said. "Did you bring your baby?"

"I put Didi in the dining room where it's quiet. She loved that darling ball you sent her, but she doesn't know her alphabet yet." Aunt Michelle chuckled. "Why don't you go see her?"

Didi was in a basket on a pink pillow. "Oh, she's beautiful!" Jessica said. She touched the shell-pink fingers with the translucent nails smaller than dewdrops. The baby's blue eyes were open. Her fine dark hair barely covered her scalp.

"You can pick her up if you like," Aunt Michelle said. "Just be careful to support her head."

Gently Jessica lifted her new cousin. The roundness of the baby's head fitted into the cup of her hand, and the butter-soft baby cheeks lifted in a crooked smile that looked so funny, it made Jessica laugh. "Hi ya, sweet stuff, how are you?" she cooed. "I'm your cousin Jes-si-ca." The little mouth worked as if it were trying to form words. "That's right, Jessica," she encouraged Didi.

"Maybe sometime this summer you could come and stay with me for a week or so if you like babies so much," Aunt Michelle said.

"Maybe. Could Tycho come, too?"

"Well, if your mother came with him, I guess that would be fine," Aunt Michelle said. "I'm sorry about your daddy, honey. He was the sweetest man in the whole world, and I know how attached you were to him. It was such a —"

"Excuse me," Jessica said. She handed her cousin back to Aunt Michelle and took off. The room she entered at random was the kitchen, and standing by the table talking to Tycho was the priest who had become Daddy's friend in Oldminesville. Daddy wouldn't join any particular religious group because he thought churches stood in the way of understanding God, but he and Father Michael had gotten to know each other from visiting the same shut-ins. "For a man of the cloth, he's pretty broad-minded," Daddy had told Mom when she asked him why he spent so much time with a priest.

Jessica put her hand on the back of her brother's chair. "Dad's not here right now," she said to Father Michael, who was a dark-haired young man with a square, tired face.

"Your father? I'd say he *is*. Where you are is where his spirit will always be, Jessica. He wouldn't leave you."

"No, he wouldn't," she agreed.

"But Mom says —" Tycho began.

"I told you Mom doesn't know everything," Jessica snapped. She turned to Father Michael, but her mind went blank. She wanted something from this man who knew about God, but she didn't know what.

"I've been thinking, Jessica," the priest said, "that since you and I are both going to be missing him, you might call me sometimes to talk about him when you feel like it. What if I give you my phone number? Think you might use it?"

Jessica shrugged and dredged up a smile for Father Michael. His tired face was kind, not the oozy kindness Jenny's mother had that forced itself on you, but a caring that was just offered. The priest fumbled for a pen and paper until Jessica handed him the notepad by the phone to use. Then he wrote a number and his name and told her it didn't matter when she called, even if it was the middle of the night, he'd be glad to hear from her.

She thanked him and left the kitchen with the piece of paper squashed in her hand. Mom was coming out of her bedroom. "Would you believe it, Jessica? His brothers' car broke down, and they asked me to hold the ceremony until they could get here tonight. I told them I just couldn't do it. There must be a couple hundred people coming." Mom wiped her dry eyes nervously. "Is Tycho ready?" she asked suddenly. "It's time to go."

Jessica looked at her in alarm. "Where?"

"To the funeral parlor, darling. I hope they have enough room for everybody. Oh, God! I wish today were over."

"I'm not going," Jessica said.

"Jessica, don't do this to me. Of course, you're going. Just stand beside me and hang on to Tycho. You don't have to talk to anyone."

"No," Jessica screamed in a panic. "No, no, no!"

In the end, they got her to the car, Alan on one side of her and her mother and Tycho on the other, but at the funeral parlor Jessica balked again. "I'm not going inside."

"Please, Jessica. Oh, please, don't give me a hard time today," Mom begged.

"Your father would want you to be brave," Alan said. And when that didn't move her, he said, "I think Tycho needs you, Jessica."

Tycho looked scared. "Jessica!" he whimpered.

Her feet began moving and she let herself be hustled along. Music was coming from somewhere in the dim room full of row after row of empty chairs. Mom walked all the way to the first row and they sat down facing a low carpeted stage. There wasn't a coffin on the stage, the way there had been when their elderly neighbor in Oldminesville had died. Except for a stand with a microphone, the stage was bare. Behind her, Jessica could hear people shuffle and scrape and cough, a murmuring crowd filling up the emptiness.

Carefully, she began reciting Daddy's favorite poem to herself. It started, "Jenny kissed me when we met, jumping from the chair she sat in . . ." but Daddy substituted her name in the poem. She recited it twice over to herself. Mom's hand felt sweaty in hers.

A man Jessica didn't know got up on the stage and made a speech about someone who had died, but Jessica didn't recognize the person. Certainly it wasn't her father, because there was nothing personal in it, just vague things about leaving a family and being so young and so well regarded in the community.

There was nothing about the bird sounds Daddy could make. Nothing about his big feet that he always mocked, or about how much he hated guns — so much that he took away the one Tycho got at a birthday party and told Tycho he could have anything else he wanted instead. Nothing about how clumsy Dad was in sports and how skillful at fixing the hurts of children and animals and machinery.

If the man were talking about Daddy, wouldn't he mention that Daddy couldn't sing very well, except for "Row, row, row your boat," which he sang with gusto in the car?

The service seemed to last forever because several of Dad's friends spoke, one after the other, but Jessica refused to listen. She sat there remembering everything she could about her father, a jumble of facts and memories, and when she ran out of material, she started figuring out where he could have gone.

After the service, Mom was halted in the aisle and almost lost to sight in the embracing arms of her school friends. Jessica grabbed hold of Tycho. Bowing her head, she hurried him through the crowd to the parking lot. The car Alan had driven them to the funeral parlor in was unlocked; she dragged Tycho inside. It was a long wait until Mom came, but Jessica didn't care. By the time they got home, Daddy might have returned. Hadn't he gone away before for conferences that lasted days? Once he and Mom had gone away on a vacation alone for a week, and Jessica had missed him worse than this.

Well, he hadn't been away for a week yet. She could stand the waiting, or she could do what she had promised Tycho and go find him — because she had finally realized where he must be.

Chapter Five

A man's strong arms were hugging Jessica. Her nose was pressed against his shirt, but the shirt didn't smell like Daddy's, and when she lifted her head in her dream to check, it was Alan's face and Alan's arms that were hugging her. She yanked herself away from him in alarm, crying out, "You're not my father!"

It was still nighttime when the dream woke her.

Outside her window, the dark began thinning into dawn. Now was the time to get ready to take Tycho to find Daddy, now before Mom woke up.

The backpack in Jessica's closet was still stuffed with spiral notebooks and school papers. She dumped them out and considered what to pack. They'd need sweaters, but they could wear those because an early June morning like this one was likely to be chilly. A storybook to read to Tycho when they stopped to rest? Too heavy to carry. Her camera wasn't heavy, but she didn't want to risk losing it on a hike where she might have to climb rocks and ford streams. No, what she really needed to pack was food.

She tiptoed down the steps to the kitchen and loaded the backpack with bread and cheese and peanut butter, a knife, and six boxes of pure fruit punch with straws attached. The pack dug into her shoulders when she tried carrying it, so she took out four juice packs and put in two paper cups instead. They should be able to get water in the picnic area on the Oldminesville side of the park.

Carrot sticks would be good, but she couldn't find them in the refrigerator, which was jammed with unfamiliar dishes of food people had brought yesterday. Instead she took two apples and two bananas from a fruit basket stuffed with shiny green imitation grass. Now the pack was as heavy as before, but she and Tycho would have enough to eat, even if the hike took all morning.

Passing through the living room on her way back upstairs, Jessica realized someone was asleep on the couch — her mother's friend Annie, judging by the spill of ginger-colored hair. Yesterday when Annie came, she had given Jessica and Tycho each a book, and burst into tears when Jessica kissed her cheek to thank her.

Even the uncles had been weepy when they finally arrived yesterday evening. "Well, kids, you know who to come to if you need anything," Uncle Pete had said with tears in his eyes. Jessica supposed he meant that they could come to him, but she couldn't imagine for what.

Uncle Martin had been nervous. He kept fidgeting with his baseball cap and rubbing his ankle and scratching his ear. "Glad school's out?" he'd asked Jessica. And when she had said yes, he said, "Nice house you got here. Better than that poky old place on the highway, huh?"

To Tycho, who was small for his age and pudgy, Uncle Martin had said, "Hey, look at those muscles. You going to be a big guy like your Daddy, huh?" Tycho had frowned at him and then looked away. He knew he took after Mom, who was hummingbird-small.

The uncles had jammed the conversational space so full of questions that little room was left for answers. It was as if they were afraid of what their niece and nephew might say. When they'd announced they couldn't spend the night because they had to get to work Monday morning, Mom acted disappointed, but Jessica had been glad to see them go.

Her parents' bedroom door was still closed. Jessica tiptoed past it cautiously and slipped into Tycho's room. "Wake up," she whispered in his ear. He rolled away from her, clutching his Bucky Baby.

"Tycho, I'm taking you to Daddy. We have to get started before Mom wakes up or she won't let us go."

Tycho scrunched down under the covers. In desperation, Jessica pinched him, but not hard enough to make him squeal. A bright pink dawn filled the sky outside his window now and she was anxious to start. He sat up rubbing his arm. "You pinched me," he accused her.

"Because," she said with an authority that had always been explanation enough for him. "Now hurry up and get dressed. And you better wear your sweater."

She eased open his chest of drawers and tossed out a tee shirt, a sweater, underpants, and socks, along with a clean pair of jeans. Thoughtfully she took an extra pair of socks to tuck in the backpack, which she'd left in the kitchen. Tycho hated walking anywhere in wet socks, and the ground was likely to be swampy in places.

What a baby he looked, sitting on the edge of his bed in his pajamas, cuddling his Bucky Baby under his chin and yawning. "You want me to help you get dressed, Tycho?" Sometimes, stuck halfway between the baby he'd been and the cool kid he wanted to be, he needed a reminder.

"I can do it," he said, as she expected. Slowly he began pulling his pajama top off over his head. At the rate he was moving, Mom would be down in the kitchen drinking her coffee before he was dressed.

"Come on, Tycho. We can't keep Daddy waiting. Hurry up."

He stopped with one arm still in his pajamas and picked up Bucky Baby again. "Daddy's dead," Tycho said. But then he asked, "Isn't he?"

"Would I be taking you to see him if he was?"

48

"But Mom said he died before he got to the hospital."

"Daddy *works* in the hospital. He helps other people get well there. Anyway," Jessica added, as she sensed a flaw in her argument, "Mom doesn't know everything, Tycho."

"She knows more than you."

"Okay, then you stay here and I'll go by myself."

"No." He hopped off the bed. "No. I'm coming." Putting on speed, he turned his back toward her and pulled off his pants. Recently he'd become modest in front of her.

"Don't forget your socks," she said and went to brush her teeth and use the toilet. If Mom caught them on their way out of the house, Jessica would say they were going for an early morning walk. That was true in a way. As for breakfast, Tycho would be happy if she gave him something sweet to munch on as they walked. Probably she could take a box of that crunchy cereal that Mom said was full of sugar, even though the box advertised, "healthy and nutritious."

"No wonder you have a gut when you eat stuff like that," Mom had told Dad when he brought the cereal back from the supermarket.

"Who has a gut?" Dad had asked, and he'd invited Tycho to punch him there to show Mom how hard it was. "That's muscle, not fat," Dad had boasted. "Why, he'll hurt his hand if he hits me too hard."

Tycho had reared back with a demonic grin and punched Dad as hard as he could. "Ooof, he got me,"

Daddy had yelled and he'd rolled on the floor, pretending to be in pain to make them all laugh.

Tycho entered the kitchen quietly. Bucky Baby was tucked under his arm, but he had on his spring jacket instead of the sweater Jessica had picked, to show her she couldn't boss him completely.

"If you take that rabbit with you, you have to carry it," Jessica said. "And if you lose it in the woods, don't expect me to waste time looking for it."

"I won't lose Bucky," Tycho said.

She gave him a glass of juice and drank one herself. He began eating the cereal dry from the box, while she considered what to write in the note she wanted to leave for Mom.

"I'm taking Tycho for a long hike. Don't worry if we're late. Love, Jessica." There, that was enough. If she mentioned where they were hiking, Mom might decide to come after them, and she was a pretty fast hiker. She'd belonged to a hiking group before she met Daddy.

Mom hiked to get to the top, not to experience the woods the way Daddy did. Tycho was the least enthusiastic hiker in the family, but he was good for a couple of miles anyway. Judging by the map that Daddy had showed her, Jessica guessed the state park that filled the valley between Oldminesville and Hammond might be two or three miles wide.

She closed the outside door quietly and put her finger to her lips to warn Tycho not to make any noise as they left. Then she hurried him through their development, but she took his hand only when they had to cross the main road. He didn't like to hold her hand when they were where other kids might see him.

Far down the road to the right was Hammond where Mom's new school and Dad's hospital were. To the left was the long way to Oldminesville. That was by car, following the roads that circled around the state park and back of the mountain and then along the highway on which postage-stamp-sized towns were spaced out. What Jessica planned to do was march straight ahead through the park and never mind the roads.

"I'm hungry," Tycho said as a bus with green windows hiding its passengers rushed by them.

"So eat some more cereal."

"I can't while I'm walking." On came his turtle look. If she didn't give in, he might decide to go home to spite her.

"Okay," she said lightly. "Let's stop and eat then." They sat on a window ledge outside a real estate sales office, next to a gas station, and finished off the cereal and the bananas.

Tycho enjoyed watching traffic. The big, bulky trucks passing them interested him. Jessica couldn't see why. She disliked the frightening get-out-of-my-way rumbles of the semis and couldn't wait to reach the quiet of the woods.

"Now I'm thirsty," Tycho said as a concrete mixer grumbled by with its drum-like body revolving rapidly.

Jessica gave him his box of juice, saving hers for later. "Let's go now," she said impatiently.

They followed a side road for a while, and then crossed the overpass above the highway and turned onto a road that passed fields and woods and even one farmhouse with a muddy yard and an old barn. Other than two horses in a paddock behind a red brick house, the only animal they saw was a dead skunk, which stank. They made a wide detour around it.

Jessica was careful to keep the sun in view. It had risen to the treetops by now.

"As the crow flies, we'll be close enough so that you could walk to Oldminesville," Daddy had said.

"Which way would a crow go?" Jessica had asked.

"Right into the morning sun across the valley through the state park. That's if he was a smart crow and in a hurry."

It hadn't comforted Jessica then to learn that they would be so close to Oldminesville, because even that close was too far. Now, though, she was thankful they could get home by walking. Home was where Daddy would be. Because where else would he go? He couldn't have just disappeared into ashes, not Daddy who had never once not been there when she needed him in the night, when she was sick, when she didn't understand something, when she wanted a hug. No way would Daddy ever not be there for her.

"How much farther, Jessica?" Tycho asked.

"We'll get to the state park soon. It starts somewhere along this road. Just keep hiking," she told him.

The last time she'd been in the state park had been in February, when Daddy had taught her to recognize the pointy pockets deer hooves made in the snow, and the dittoed pattern of rabbits' feet. Of course, that had been on the Oldminesville side.

They kept walking without getting anywhere as if they were on an endless treadmill. She began to be less sure of their direction even though she'd been along this road in a car. She wished she had packed Daddy's map. The place looked different on foot. But, she consoled herself, there was more to see on foot, like that tiny blue butterfly on a blossoming weed. It was just taking them much longer than she had expected.

"There." Jessica stopped short. "Those might be the right kind of trees." She had forgotten what Daddy called them. They were tall and dark with tiny needles that stayed on all winter.

"But Jessica," Tycho said, leaping out at her from the middle of his thoughts, "if Daddy's not dead, how come those people kept talking about him?"

"What people?"

"You know, yesterday when Mom made you go where all the chairs were."

"They didn't say anything about *our* daddy," she snapped, horrified that Tycho should recognize their father in the vague description of some young man who had been "taken before his time" and had left "a grieving widow and two young children." "That man who talked first didn't even *know* our daddy. So how could he say anything about him?"

"Well, but he said his name."

"He said Bob. Our daddy's name was Robbie. You know that."

"But Mom was there. And everybody —"

"Do you want to go home now?" she interrupted him to demand. "If you don't want to come with me, just turn around and go home by yourself."

He straightened up indignantly. "You *know* I can't cross streets by myself, Jessica."

He had her there. Angry tears came to her eyes. "All right then, I'll take you back," she said. "I thought you could keep up with me and we could do things together. Well, I guess you're just a baby still. Let's go." She started back the way they had come.

"Okay, okay," Tycho relented. "You don't have to get so mad. I'm coming. I was just asking because —"

"Because nothing," she said to shut him up.

She did an about-face and walked stiffly across the field toward the dark patch of evergreens, not even looking behind to be sure he was following. There was a fence at the back of the field made of wood posts with wire strung in such a way that only a small animal could get through. In silence Jessica paced along the fence, hoping to find a break in it. When she finally saw a tree trunk that had toppled onto the fence, making a natural bridge over it, it was like a sign, like an invitation.

Balancing with some difficulty, Jessica led Tycho over the bridge. Mom had been a gymnast in high school and she had wanted Jessica to take lessons, but Jessica hadn't been good on the balance beam; she had gotten dizzy when she was upside-down. "Like father like daughter," Dad had said. Now Mom was going to try Tycho at gymnastics — maybe this summer. She said he might be good at it because he took after her.

Who cares? Jessica thought. She was good at other things, like nursing for instance. She'd kept that baby rabbit alive with the medicine dropper until it could manage outside by itself, hadn't she? And Mom had predicted the rabbit would die after Mimsy had killed its mother. Instead it was Mimsy who died. . . . Daddy hadn't let her see the body. He'd just handed her the shoebox, tied up and heavy, and helped her bury it in the pet cemetery, where his old dog was buried near the climbing tree.

In the grove, the evergreens were so tall that Jessica could no longer see the sun. Although she set off determinedly, she wasn't sure about her direction. The trees went straight up higher than a house to an intertwining of branches. Nothing much grew beneath them, but the brown, spicy-smelling needles made the ground soft underfoot.

She heard a woodpecker knocking and noted a place where one tree was leaning on another. The broken-off roots stuck up in the air. "There are no street signs to guide you in the woods," Daddy had said. "You have to be sharp-eyed and notice little differences so that if you get lost and start circling, you can recognize where you've been before."

She was fixing the dead tree in her mind when Tycho startled her by saying, "You think it's a trick, don't you?" He sounded as if he had figured out something that finally made sense to him.

"What's a trick?"

"That Daddy's dead."

"He's not dead and will you stop talking about it? *Please!*" she said with angry emphasis. "You make me crazy when you talk about it."

"But Jessica —"

"Shut up," she said. The nastiness stopped him. She didn't care if she was being mean. For two days now she had felt as if she were dodging a mugger who stalked her no matter which way she turned. Every time Tycho mentioned Daddy, the mugger threatened her. And she was getting tired. It terrified her that she might not duck or hide in time. Then the mugger would get her, and she would suffocate with fear.

To Jessica's relief, they emerged from the grove of small-needled evergreens onto a high bank. Below them was a wide, safe-looking stream. She could see fist-sized flat rocks on its bottom, which meant it was shallow. There weren't any little rushes of white water either to indicate a fast current.

"Let's take our shoes and socks off," Jessica said. She

pulled off hers, slid down the bank, and stepped into the water.

"Yeow, it's cold!" Tycho exclaimed. He was testing the water with his bare toes.

"Roll your pants legs up higher so they don't get wet," she advised him as she kept going to reach the opposite bank.

Here, besides the sprinkling of dark evergreens, were other kinds of trees. Some had smooth or straight ridged bark. On other trunks the bark was diamond-patterned, or loose and shaggy. Columns of sunlight pierced the lacy lattice of leaves, and when the breeze shook them the shadows danced. It was like a tree garden, Jessica thought.

"See the birch," she said. "That's the kind the Indians made their canoes out of."

"I know that," Tycho said wearily.

She picked up a coil of loose birchbark and began ripping narrow ribbons from it to drop behind them as a marker for their path — just in case. At times like these she wished Tycho were old enough so that she didn't always have to be the big sister, responsible for his safety. If Daddy were here, she could walk through this woods leaving him to worry about which way to go. Even though she made the pieces of birchbark smaller and smaller, she soon ran out of material for marking the trail.

An amber-colored chipmunk with a black and white striped back was sitting on a rock ahead of them, glistening prettily in the sunlight. "Look!" Jessica cried as the chipmunk leaped for a nearby tree.

The sun was still in front of them as they came upon another stream, narrower and with weedy islands in it. "Let's look for lizards," Tycho said.

"Okay," she agreed cheerfully. "But what are you going to do if you find one?"

"Take it home with me."

"We don't have anything to carry it in, Tycho." But to keep from ruining his fun, she suggested, "Maybe we could use a paper cup. I brought two. And you could put moss in. The salamander should live until we get back home." She meant to Oldminesville.

"Okay. Okay. But we didn't catch any yet. Help me, Jessica."

"Bucky's falling out of your pocket," she told him.

Without a pause, Tycho pulled off his spring jacket and dumped it and Bucky on the bank. It was getting too warm for a jacket anyway. Jessica took off her sweater and stuffed it in the pack.

When she saw the finger-sized fish circling in the shade of an overhanging bush, she said, "How about a fish instead of a salamander?" She used one of the cups as a scoop and caught two narrow brown fish. "Look, aren't they cute?"

"But I want the kind of salamander that turns red."

They searched until Tycho suddenly stiffened and pointed, saying hoarsely, "Jessica." She turned and saw something moving on the bank, a snake, a mass of snakes. They were undulating on the mossy bank in the sunlight like long, thin vines.

"Let's get out of the stream," Jessica said, and she moved hastily to the opposite bank.

"They can't hurt us, can they?" Tycho asked.

"No. They're just garter snakes or something like that. But you don't want to step on one if it decides to take a swim, do you?"

Tycho shook his head and joined her on the bank. "I'm thirsty again."

She divided the container of juice by pouring half of it into the second cup. They finished the drink off in a few swallows. She wished she had brought water. Drinking the stream water wouldn't be safe. Daddy never let her drink the water in streams he didn't know.

"We could have lunch here if you want," she said.

"Is it lunchtime? Did we walk all morning?"

She looked at the sun angling through the trees. "No, it's not twelve o'clock yet. That's when the sun's right overhead." And then she wouldn't be able to tell which way to go, she realized with a jolt of fear.

"Maybe we ought to keep walking until it's noon, Tycho," she said. She had expected they'd be in Old-minesville by now. They must be getting close. She hoped they didn't have much farther to go through the woods.

Mom was going to be really worried about them. As soon as they got to Oldminesville, Jessica would ask a neighbor if she could use the phone to call home. "We're fine," she'd reassure her mother. "I'm sorry we scared you. We're in Oldminesville."

Mom would be impressed. "What are you doing there?" she'd ask.

"Finding Daddy," Jessica would say. Probably Mom wouldn't understand. "He didn't want to move," Jessica would say. "You made him so you wouldn't have to drive far to work." And because Mom didn't like the old-fashioned kitchen, and the basement was just a crawl space, and the bathroom had a leaky wall and pipes that froze in the winter.

"We could fix up the old place," Daddy had told Mom, but she didn't want to. It hadn't been home to her. But it was home to Daddy. His climbing tree was there. And Jessica felt certain he would be there, too.

Chapter Six

The sun that shone on the slab of rock Jessica had chosen for their picnic enclosed them in a drowsy warmth. Tycho yawned and lay down with his head on his arms. A nap would do him good, Jessica thought as she repacked the leftover bread and peanut butter from their lunch. In fact, she wouldn't mind a nap herself. Before closing her eyes, she carefully fixed in her mind the dead tree riddled with woodpecker holes across the ravine. That was the way they had to go.

When she woke up, the sun still seemed to be right overhead. "Wake up, Tycho," she said. "We better get through this park fast or Mom's going to be very, very worried." Not to mention angry at Jessica.

"Are we lost?" Tycho asked.

"Uh uh. See that dead tree at the top of the ridge? From there, we should spot a road or something."

"I wish we'd see a water fountain. I'm thirsty."

Since she couldn't satisfy his thirst, Jessica ignored his remark and said what Daddy always told them, "Make sure you pick up everything and leave only your footsteps behind."

At first she thought Tycho's eyes were widening because she had reminded him of Daddy, but then Tycho said, "My Bucky! He's in my jacket, and I lost it."

He looked around wildly, but Jessica knew instantly where the jacket was. In her mind she could see it lying beside the stream where they'd hunted for the salamander. How far back was the stream from where they were now? Half a mile? A quarter of a mile? Anyway, too far to risk backtracking to find it.

"I know where Bucky is," Jessica said, "but we can't go back for him now, Tycho, or we'll never get to Old-minesville. I told you not to take him, didn't I?"

Large fat tears promptly rolled down his cheeks. The hopeless silence of his crying made her squirm. "All right. All right," she said. "I'll tell you what. Soon as we can, we'll call Mom to pick us up, and then, tomorrow, we'll go back for Bucky to that stream where you left him."

Tycho shook his head, scattering tears.

"We can't get him now," she argued. "Don't worry. He'll be safe. No one's going to take him."

"I want to go home."

"Oh, Tycho, don't be such a baby."

"I don't care. I want to go *hoooooome*." He stood up, squeezed his eyes shut and screamed, "Mom! Mommy!"

Jessica tried to reason with him. "Mom can't hear you. We're practically in Oldminesville already. It's dumb to give up now, Tycho."

It took a while until he cried himself out, and when he finally gave in and agreed to let Bucky wait, the sun had gone behind a cloud. Jessica set out confidently toward the dead tree with Tycho lagging behind her. He looked unhappy, but the tears had stopped.

The view from the ridge punctured her courage. Below them, as far as she could see, was nothing but more trees. No signs of human presence relieved the endless green of the woods — no roads, no water fountains, no picnic tables, not even litter. And now, with the clouds hiding the sun, Jessica didn't know which way to go. "Uh oh," she said while her eyes searched desperately for a clue.

"You're lost, aren't you?" Tycho's accusing tone stiffened her spine.

"No, I'm not. I only said *maybe* we'd see something from here. It's always farther than you think when you're looking for a place, and shorter on the way back." Another quote from Daddy's woods lore. "Come on. Let's hurry."

She strode ahead purposely, barely noticing the chickadees fee-beeing overhead, or the patch of jacks-in-the-pulpit that would have delighted her if she hadn't been so anxious about where they were.

"There's that tree again," Tycho said about an hour later.

She saw the dead tree that the woodpeckers had pockmarked and sank to the ground in despair. They must have circled somehow, and considering how tired she felt, Tycho had to be exhausted. He sat down beside her, but rather than complain, he just said calmly, "I told you you were lost."

"Am not," she said and burst into tears. It wasn't fair. She had done everything right, everything Daddy taught her, and he had said she was a good woodsperson — getting to be good anyway. Then why was she lost? And where was Daddy? She couldn't remember a time when he hadn't appeared to help her, to hold her and hug her and make what was wrong right again. Always, just when she needed him, he'd appeared.

Tycho touched her shoulder and began timidly patting her back. "Don't cry, Jessica. I'm sorry. You're not lost. I know you're not."

"Yes, I am," she confessed. "I don't know which way to go next, Tycho."

"Well . . ." He considered. "Maybe we should just sit here until they find us."

It sounded like a reasonable suggestion. She took a few deep breaths to calm herself while she thought it over. But then she said, "Until who finds us? Nobody knows where we went."

"Oh, yeah."

"We have to get ourselves out of here. We've got to just keep walking, Tycho."

She stood up and stretched on tiptoe, peering past tree

trunks in all directions. But when they were at this dead tree before, hadn't they stood on a ridge and looked down on treetops? And those bushes that looked like arched thorny wands with little leaves — they hadn't been here before, had they? "I don't think this is the same dead tree," she said. "Maybe we're *not* walking in circles."

He shrugged and waited for her to decide what to do next. She tried to think. A squirrel ran across a branch over her head and stopped to scold them. It kept flicking its gray tail and chattering at them in a rackety voice. "Be quiet," Jessica told it. "It's not our fault we're here." But it was her fault. She was the big sister, and she'd led the way.

Jessica stuck the back of her finger in her mouth and bit it. An army of faceless brown tree trunks stood at attention around her. Any minute they might advance, and how could she and Tycho escape them? She fought down panic and said, "Come on, Tycho. Let's go that way." She pointed at random and tramped off recklessly over the leaf-littered earth, trusting to luck to lead her.

A few minutes later she spotted a pile of small rocks. "Let's stack up some rocks so we can recognize this place," Jessica said.

"Why? Are we coming back here?"

"Well, not that we want to, but if we do by accident, at least we'll know we've been here."

"I wish I had my Bucky Baby," Tycho said, but he

helped her pick three rocks that would balance one on top of the other.

They descended another slope and walked through a bed of ferns. Easy enough to remember these, Jessica thought, although she regretted crushing them. For a minute, she considered unraveling her sweater and leaving pieces of the wool on branches. But if they didn't get out of the woods by nightfall, they'd need the sweater, especially since it was the only warm garment they had now.

The clouds had curdled into a lumpy gray coating low over their heads. Rain was coming. "Want some peanut butter?" Jessica asked her brother. It was the only good thing she had to offer him.

"Okay." Sad faced, he leaned against a tree, scooping up peanut butter with his finger and licking it off. Suddenly he slumped to a sitting position on the ground. Jessica braced herself to hear more complaints about their being lost, but what he said was, "Anyway, Mom might get me a video game for my birthday now."

"What do you mean 'now'?" Did he mean now they had moved or now he was older or some other now to do with their father? To ward him off in case it had to do with their father, she said, "You always want junk, and then after you get it, you don't play with it."

"Video games aren't junk."

"They're boring. Chasing and shooting. That's all they are."

"Just because you don't like them doesn't make them

junk," Tycho said. "Anyway, everybody's got one."

"Not everybody. Just that kid in school who has an older brother."

"I wish *I* had a brother."

"Daddy'll get you one when you're old enough."

"But if he doesn't come back?"

Coldly she said, "Come back from where? He didn't go anywhere."

"Yes, he did, Jessica." Instead of meeting her eyes he stared at his toes and muttered, "He's dead and you just won't admit it."

"Mommy's baby!" she screamed at him in outrage. "Every time you want something, you go to Mommy because she gives baby Tycho anything he wants. But Daddy's trying to raise you right. He knows what's good for you."

"You're mean," Tycho said.

"I'm not mean." For him to be so calm when she was collapsing into screaming bits upset her so much she began to quiver. "You like Mommy best, *don't* you?"

"So? You like Daddy best."

With an effort, she steadied herself and made her voice normal as she said, "Tycho, you be a good brother and I'll be a good sister, okay? . . . Because we need to keep going."

"But we're not getting anywhere."

"Well, we're not going in circles because we don't come back to things, so we must be getting to somewhere."

It wasn't a very solid argument, but it was enough to satisfy him. At least he followed as she trudged on. Surely they had walked miles and miles, ten maybe — longer anyway than any hike they'd ever done with their parents. If Daddy were here, he'd be giving Tycho a piggyback ride. He'd always done that for Jessica, too, when she was small enough to be toted.

It would even be wonderful if Mom appeared now. Jessica was done being angry at Mom for making her listen to that man pretending to be sad about somebody he didn't even know. Surely, if he'd known Daddy, he'd have told how wild birds quieted when Daddy held them, or how Daddy's deep voice hummed like music, or how Daddy could touch the ceiling without using a chair. If he'd really been talking about Daddy, he'd have mentioned the time Daddy whooped like a kid on his old toboggan going down the hill with Tycho and her. And how when she was little, Daddy had teased her, saying the moon must like her because it was watching her through the car window all the way home.

No way would the Robbie Turner she knew die on her, not when she was still a child and needed him.

When they finally saw the hut below them, at the bottom of the hill, Jessica was so dizzy from weariness she almost didn't believe it. But Tycho said, "Look, Jessica." He was staring at the roof, which was camouflaged with evergreen branches and clumps of dried mud and grass.

From anywhere else they might not have seen the

place at all because it was tucked into the hillside and hedged around with bushes. A cooking pot hung over the fire burning inside a ring of stones a few feet from the hut. The pot was held up by an iron pipe, propped up at either end by tripods of thick branches. The meaty smell coming from the pot made Jessica's stomach squeeze on its own emptiness. It had to be near dinnertime.

Overhead, dark clouds rumbled. "The first thing we have to do is call Mom," Jessica said.

Light-footed in her relief that help was at hand, she began scrambling down the hillside, which was steep enough so that she had to grab hold of little trees and whatever else would keep her from sliding pell-mell onto the roof.

She ended upright on the ground beside the secret hut. It looked like something a child had patched together of found materials. She hoped it wasn't just a child's shack. They needed an adult badly. The thump behind her was Tycho. He had landed right on the roof.

"Oops!" Jessica said, pressing her fingers to her mouth, but the roof held firm.

Tycho was sitting on it, getting his bearings, when the door of the hut flew open. An old woman came out with a rifle in her hands. She waved it around wildly, then settled her aim right at Tycho.

"That's my brother," Jessica said shrilly. "He didn't mean anything. He just fell."

The old woman turned to stare at her, blinking as if

she were having a hard time focusing. "Who are you?" she asked in a hoarse voice. She didn't have any teeth in her sunken-in mouth and gray hair straggled out from a braid. She looked so much like a witch that Jessica was scared. But witches were only in fairy tales.

Taking a deep breath, Jessica said, "I'm Jessica and this is my brother Tycho."

"You get out of here," the woman said. "Scoot, and don't you tell no one you was here or I'll blast you full of holes."

"Are you an outlaw?" Tycho asked.

That made the old woman grin. "You got it, kid," she said. "An outlaw. That's me."

The grin gave Jessica hope. "Please," she begged, "we need help." Before she could explain further that they were lost and needed to use the phone, the gun barrel swung her way and she caught her breath in fear again.

"I can't help you," the old woman said in dead earnest. "I can't help nobody, not even myself. Now get out of here."

Jessica didn't move. She had never met an adult like this one, and she didn't know what to do next.

Chapter Seven

Just as Jessica was ready to bolt for the safety of the woods, Tycho piped up with, "That's not a real gun. Anyway, it's broken."

"What do you mean broken?" the woman sputtered. She set the gun butt on the ground and, holding the tip at arm's length, leaned back to study it. Her comical stance cured Jessica's fear. Almost. The stump-shaped woman's baggy pants and heavy man's jacket still seemed suspiciously odd for this warm summer evening.

"How did you know that so fast?" the woman asked Tycho.

"Because. See the barrel?" Tycho slid off the roof. He trotted over to the gun, and pointed to where half the metal part that should have held the bullets was missing.

Jessica flushed with pride in him. His keen observation had literally disarmed the old woman.

"Shows how much I know about guns," she said

gruffly. "I found this one. Thought it would do to scare off trespassers. Like *you*." She glared at Tycho and then at Jessica in a threatening way.

"We weren't doing anything wrong," Jessica said in case the threat was really meant.

"Well, but I got to be on guard. They find where I'm at and soon enough they'll come round giving me trouble. It's being old. They think they can do what they want with me. But I'm not as decrepit as they think." The woman thumped the ground with the rifle butt for emphasis. "I'm managing good. Even Alf could see that when he found me here. Don't need nobody. Got my little friends, too. Just leave me alone is all I ask."

Birdsong poured into the silence while they stood there eyeing each other in a moment of indecision. "If I could just your phone to call my mother —" Jessica began.

The old woman laughed, open-mouthed, a hearty laugh that left her face in happy creases. "Honey, this ain't civilization you stumbled into. This is an outpost and I am an outlaw. Got no phone. Got nothing here that you might want. Unless you're hungry."

"*I* am," Tycho said. He looked at the pot hanging over the fire and sniffed deeply of the meaty smell coming from it.

"Well, you can have some stew with me then," the woman said. "I'm used to dinner guests. Get a lot of them." She nodded with a sly grin as if she had made a joke. "Don't have much in the way of crockery to feed you off of, though, but you can make do. Just wait here." She went into her hut and closed the door behind her.

Immediately Jessica moved to Tycho's side and whispered into his ear. "Don't eat anything here. You don't know what she's cooking. We'll just ask her how to get out of here and go. It can't be far to Oldminesville now."

"My name's Tilda," the woman said, coming out with one plate, two bowls, a fork, and two spoons. "Here." She handed them each a bowl, gave a fork to Jessica and a spoon to Tycho.

"Thank you," Jessica said. "But really you don't need to feed us. If you'll just tell us how to get to Oldminesville — We've been lost all day, and our mother must be really worried about us."

"Sit down, sit down," Tilda said. "I got to think about this because it's a problem, see? If I tell you how to get out, then you could tell them how to get in, and then I wouldn't be an outlaw no more. Then I'd be just another one of the poor old souls they got locked up in that place. Some of them don't even know their own name and they smell because — No, I'm not taking a chance of ending up back there." She looked at Jessica apologetically. "I'm sorry about your mother."

"But we wouldn't tell anybody where you are. Honestly we wouldn't," Jessica said.

"No." Tilda shook her head. "No, I'm sorry. I just can't take a chance."

"You could blindfold us and lead us through the

woods to Oldminesville and then we wouldn't know how to get back," Tycho said. "I saw that on TV once."

"You did? Boy, you are smart to think of that!" Tilda said. "I guess that TV *is* good for something besides bad news and junk." Again she gave her hearty, open-mouthed laugh.

Tycho smiled. Even Jessica smiled. "Would you do that?" she asked Tilda. "I mean, blindfold us and lead us out."

"Might. I have to think about it," Tilda said. "Meanwhile, you better have some stew. Got too much. I always cook too much, and then sometimes my little friends don't like it and it's wasted."

"Who are your little friends?" Tycho asked.

"You'll see. Stay a while and you'll meet them. . . . Never had too much food when my four boys was growing up. They'd eat whatever I put out and more. Seems that's what mothering was mainly — cooking and serving and being left with their dirty dishes when they run off to football practice or their jobs. They was always rushing off somewhere. And then they left me for good, all but Alf."

"Alf's a funny name," Tycho said.

"Tycho!" Jessica admonished.

But the old woman didn't seem angry. She said, "You think so? It's short for Alfred. That was my daddy's name. Well, my daddy's been dead forty years now, and Alf, he's married and has kids. His wife and me don't get along too good." Tilda shrugged. "She's got her ways and I've got mine, and who's to say hers aren't better." She nodded to herself and went to dish up the stew.

Tycho was staring at the hut. "Did four boys *all* sleep here?" he asked. It barely seemed big enough for one bed.

Tilda's doughy face wrinkled into laugh lines again, and she patted Tycho's head. "No, we had a regular house, the boys and me," she said. "Alf's got it now, him and the gal he married and her kids. . . . The deal was they was supposed to take care of me. . . . Well, I should have known better than to expect they would. You got to stand on your own in this world and live the best you can."

Tilda nodded again in agreement with her own thought. "They had me in my own room, the big front bedroom," she continued, "until Alf moved me into that place. His wife said I needed folks my own age to keep me company. I told him not me. I like being alone. Don't need nobody. Especially not strangers who can't do for themselves no more. Alf said there wasn't noplace else, but I remembered this shack the boys built, and I snuck out one night and come here."

She chuckled to herself. "Took Alf weeks before he thought where to look for me. 'You take me back to that so-called home for old folks and I'll die,' I told him. 'I can take care of myself,' I said. 'Strong as an ox and never needed a doctor in my life.' Finally got him convinced to leave me be here. But it's a secret. Nobody knows but Alf and me."

"My sister's strong," Tycho said. "So's my daddy."

Tilda smiled at him. She said, "You will be too, I bet." And she asked companionably, "So how did you get here?"

"We were trying to cross the state park from Hammond to get to Oldminesville where my father is," Jessica said. "We started out this morning, and we've been lost all day."

"Oh, my!" Tilda said. "Must have been scary being lost in the woods."

"It was," Tycho said with conviction.

"Well, I'll think about that blindfold idea." The old woman shook her head as if she had her doubts about it. "Meanwhile, find yourself a seat." She gestured with a gnarled root of a hand at the tree stumps around the fire that apparently served her as chairs and table.

Jessica sat on a stump and Tycho settled onto another.

"What did you say your names was?"

Jessica told her.

The old woman nodded and introduced herself again. "My name's Matilda," she said. "You could call me Tilda, or you could call me Granny if you want. I got grandchildren. Haven't seen them much. They didn't like to visit me in the home. Alf felt bad about it. He knew it wasn't right, but his wife — Well, that's water under the dam. He comes by now and then and brings me stuff."

She gave them their bowls of stew. Tycho echoed Jessica's thanks.

"It smells good," Jessica said, but she was wondering if it was safe to eat. The brown chunks were probably meat, and that orange piece had to be a carrot. Carrots were ordinary enough. Tilda had dished some stew out for herself and was eating it slowly from a spoon. If she was eating it, it should be all right, Jessica reasoned. Her mouth watered. It was definitely dinnertime or past it, and she was hungry. She ate. The stew tasted fine.

"Could I have some water, please?" Tycho asked Tilda politely.

Tilda nodded. "I have a big jar. Fill it when it rains. And I have cans of juice."

"Tycho would like juice if you please," Jessica said quickly. Jars filled when it rained didn't sound safe to her.

"Juice it is," Tilda said cheerfully. She disappeared into the hut.

"She's a pretty nice lady," Tycho said. "I wish we had a grandma like her."

"But I don't know if she's going to show us the way out of here," Jessica said.

Tilda reappeared. "Here's a can," she said. "I think it's apple juice. The store gives me cans where the label's gone." She used a beer can opener to make two triangular holes in the top of the large can. Tipping her head back, she drank from one of the holes. "Tastes good anyways. Here," she said, handing the can over to Tycho. He set his cup down on the stump and stood up to take the can in both hands.

"It's too big for you, Tycho. Use our cup," Jessica said quickly. "Wait." She slipped the nearly empty backpack from her shoulders to get out the paper cups.

"I can do it," Tycho said. He raised the can and drank from one of the openings to prove the can wasn't too heavy for him. Jessica watched him in dismay, hoping it wasn't the same side Tilda had used. The danger of germs was something Mom had drilled into Jessica.

"Here comes my next guest," Tilda said.

A triangular head, marked with a black mask, appeared atop a pair of paws over the edge of one of Tilda's stumps. "A raccoon!" Jessica cooed in delight.

"Hush now. You sit still so's you don't frighten him." Tilda held out a carrot end with the greens still on it.

Jessica was wondering where the animal had come from when she saw another coon, a large one the size of a spaniel, behind Tilda. It reached into a pocket of Tilda's loose sweater and took out a whitish tuber.

"This is the mama," Tilda said of the large coon who was sitting on the ground right beside her, turning the food round and round in her front paws as she chewed it down rapidly. "Her and me made friends, and when she got a family, she brought them round to meet me. Didn't you, Mrs. Coony?"

"The coons are your friends?" Jessica asked.

"Coons and chipmunks and mice. The mice are little pests, but I like watching them, so I let them get away with chewing up my old boots. Could've used them boots in the mud this spring, but what're you going to do? You like wild animals, girl?"

"Jessica loves all kinds of animals," Tycho said. "Daddy and she made a hospital in the basement. They took care of rabbits, like when Jessica's cat caught them. And they had a baby bird."

"He was just a starling," Jessica said.

"I took care of a crow once," Tilda said. "Soon's he got the use of his wing back, he took to swooping down on the boys while they rode their bicycles. Scared the pants off of the insurance man when he flew down and stole the little feather from the man's hat. And don't think that bird didn't know what a funny fellow he was. Used to cock his head and laugh right back at me. But he left me too." Tilda nodded as if in agreement with her own thoughts.

"Or someone shot him," she continued. "Anyways, he took off one spring and I never saw him again. Mrs. Coony here, she's the faithful type." Tilda offered the coon what was left in her bowl, but the animal sniffed it and backed away.

There were four coons in the clearing now, two very small ones and the one that was half the size of the large Mrs. Coony. Tilda seemed to have endless scraps in her pocket. It intrigued Jessica to see how boldly even the two little coons approached the old woman for food. They spent more time tussling and rolling each other around in a furry ball than eating, though.

"I wish I had a pet coon," Jessica said.

"Don't make good pets. They got to be in the woods free to come and go. Pen them up and they get mean." Tilda laughed shortly and added, "Like me. Anyways, you wouldn't want to get your fingers bitten. They got strong teeth."

It was dark by the time Jessica had tempted one coon, the medium-sized one she had first seen, to take a bit of lettuce leaf from her fingers. He reached for the leaf with his hand-like paws, stretching up on tiptoe for it.

Tycho had long since lost interest in the coons. He was whittling a stick with the kitchen knife he'd taken from Jessica's pack.

"What're you going to make of that?" Tilda asked him.

"I don't know."

"Give it here, and I'll show you something," Tilda said. He gave her the stick, and she brought another knife out of one of her cavernous pockets. Working at the knobby end of the stick, she deftly fashioned the head of a raccoon. "There," she said. "Now you got something useful."

"That's neat," Tycho said with sincere admiration. "But what can I use it for?"

Tilda chuckled at his question. "Why, you can give it to your sister for her birthday. She likes coons." Smiling, she looked like someone's kindly great-grandmother.

The blackness was speckled with stars overhead. "I

bet it's past Tycho's bedtime. We should get home," Jessica said.

"Too late to go anywhere tonight. I'll put you up and tomorrow we'll see. I don't know about leading you, though. Even if you mean not to tell, it's bound to slip out. Then they'll come looking and sure enough they'll find me, and I'll be right back in that place." Tilda shook her head. "I don't know."

She rose stiffly. "Anyways, it's time to go to bed." She collected her dishes and wiped them off with leaves. "Clean them up tomorrow," she said. The raccoons had disappeared. As if to make matters worse, thunder rumbled far off and a sudden spatter of raindrops hit them.

"Jessica!" Tycho said in alarm. She put her arms around him as much to comfort herself as him. Then she pulled her sweater from the pack and wrapped it around Tycho. They both flinched at a loud crack of thunder.

"Better get inside before it pours," Tilda said. She held open the door to her hut and let them in. A candle inside a can threw moving shadows on the rough wood walls. Tilda's bed took up half the room. A table and an armchair and something that looked like an iron stove took up the other half. A rag rug lay on the floor in the middle.

"You can take the chair and the boy can sleep on the rug," Tilda said. "I'll give you each a blanket. I don't need this whole pile anymore. Want the blue satin quilt that my mama gave me when I got married? It's the prettiest." Tilda put her fingers over her lips, losing herself inside her own thoughts.

Quietly Jessica asked, "Is there a bathroom?"

"Outhouse," Tilda said shortly. "I'll show you where it is."

It was on the other side of the hut, hidden in the bushes, and it smelled. Jessica tried not to breathe while she used it. She wondered what Tilda did about brushing her teeth and then remembered she didn't have any. The old woman could probably wash in a stream, but where did she get her food? Her son might bring it, but she had said something about a store giving her cans without labels, hadn't she? And if she went to a store, it probably wasn't more than a mile or two away. But how could they get her to give them directions to it?

Jessica felt her way back to the hut and took her place in the chair, wrapping the threadbare satin quilt around herself reluctantly. It might have been pretty once, but it wasn't anymore, and it didn't smell clean. Nothing in Tilda's hut did. But it was warm. Jessica rubbed her eyes. Her weighted eyelids kept closing on her.

Tycho was curled on the rug under the blanket Tilda had lent him. Now, with his eyes closed, he popped his thumb in his mouth. Baby, Jessica thought. And yet he'd been a help with Tilda. Jessica lifted her eyelids with effort and concentrated on keeping them up so that she could plan tomorrow. But her mind wouldn't take hold.

She willed her father to come, and convinced herself that any minute he'd appear to save them. He'd carry her home and put her down in her own clean, soft bed. Then life would be the way it was just last week, just a few days ago — before he had gone out to get the ice cream.

For the first time, Jessica wondered if she should have gone with him. If she had gone, would everything have turned out differently?

"Daddy," she mouthed silently. "Daddy, oh Daddy, I need you so bad."

She caught her lower lip in her teeth. What had Tilda said? "You got to stand on your own and live the best you can." But what if you were a kid, and what if you weren't ready?

Chapter Eight

Jessica was startled into wakefulness. Someone was moaning. She was in a dark cold place and her shoulder and neck and back ached from sleeping sitting up. In the same instant that the cry rose in her throat, she realized where she was and jammed her fist against her mouth to silence herself.

The old woman, Tilda, was thrashing around in her bed yelling, "Get away from me. Get. Get away from me. No, no, *Maaama!*" The "Mama" was the long-drawn-out scream of a terror-stricken child. It was eerie to hear someone so old crying for her mother. Tilda's mother had to have died long ago and Tilda must be dreaming. Now she was whimpering pitifully in her dream. Jessica shuddered and stood up.

Relieved to find herself fully dressed in yesterday's clothes, she picked up the backpack, which had been squeezed against her side, and took a step. Her foot touched Tycho on the rug. She crouched and put her arms around him, whispering his name.

"I'm awake," he surprised her by saying in a normal voice. Then she felt how he was shivering.

"Let's get out of here," she said. She took his hand and felt her way to the door with her other hand. It was growing light outside. In fact, she could see the blush of dawn above the screen of bushes and trees that were still beaded with droplets of last night's rain. "There," she said to Tycho. "That's the way we have to go."

"But shouldn't we say good-bye to Tilda?"

"What if we wait for her and she decides not to help us?"

"She wouldn't keep us here," he said.

"Maybe not, but who knows what she'll do, and while we can see the sun rising, we know the way to Oldminesville by ourselves."

"Okay," he argued, "but she fed us and gave us a place to sleep."

"Yes, she did." Jessica considered. He meant they owed Tilda a thank-you, and he was right. If only she had paper and pencil, she could write a note, but she didn't — and her urge to leave was too strong. Already the pink glow was fading.

Impatiently, Jessica said, "Come on, Tycho. We have to get out of here now. We have to. We'll write to Tilda later. Let's go."

She set off across the small clearing where Tilda had entertained them and the raccoons. Tycho followed on her heels without further argument. A quick scan of the damp, leafy floor, and Jessica thought she detected a faint path leading toward a large boulder. At the boulder, the slightly compressed look of the ground sent her to the left. The ground began rising. Part of it became a steep bank. They climbed, clinging to tree roots, and circled upward until they reached the top of the bank. But now Jessica didn't see anything resembling a path in any direction.

One wisp of pink-tinted cloud remained like a signpost in the morning sky. She plunged wildly through the prickery underbrush toward it and when it was gone, she fixed her eye on the delicate pale lace of a tree that seemed to have leafed out later than the ones around it. By the time she and Tycho were at the tree, Jessica was out of breath, and Tycho was begging her to slow up.

"I can't run so fast," he told her indignantly when he'd gotten his breath.

She inhaled and waited for her heartbeat to quiet down as she stared toward what she hoped was east, the east of the rising sun. Now that the sky was just a wash of blue and the sun was hidden behind the trees, she couldn't be sure. In the woods around them, the birds were going about their morning activities, calling to each other in cheerful trills and peeps as they dipped from branch to branch. This was their home, but it wasn't hers or Tycho's. Discouragement settled like an ache into Jessica's bones. "I don't know if we're ever going to get out of this place," she said.

"We could go back and ask Tilda to help us," Tycho said.

"No."

"Why not?"

"Because."

"You always say 'because.' Well, I don't care, Jessica. I'm going back and ask her."

"No, don't," Jessica said in alarm. "You don't know about her. She'd rather live in a shack alone in the woods than in a home for old people. What if she's a little crazy?"

"Well, you're crazy, and I trust you."

He looked too serious to be joking. "Me? What do you mean? I'm not crazy."

"Yes, you are." Tycho frowned at her, looking remarkably like their mother when she was calling Jessica to account. "Daddy's dead. Mommy said so. But you say he's in Oldminesville. And that's how we got into this woods. And I don't think we can get out by ourselves."

She crumpled to the ground as if he'd punched her. Was she crazy? Was Daddy really dead, gone where she could never see him again, never touch him — never? A terrible pain gripped her chest. She moaned, hugging herself. When she finally stopped, Tycho said guiltily, "I'm sorry."

"I'm sorry, too," she cried. She had gotten him into this. "I'm sorry, Tycho, really." She reached out her arms to him, and he let himself be hugged briefly.

When she was done hugging him, he asked, "Is there any peanut butter left?"

"Sure." Grateful to have something to give him, she offered him the peanut butter jar. Along with a couple of pieces of stale bread and the knife and soggy paper cups, it was all that remained in the backpack. They ate peanut butter sandwiches for breakfast and repacked the empty jar rather than litter the woods with it.

Once the edge was off her hunger, Jessica felt more hopeful. "We'll just keep walking," she said, taking charge again. "And maybe we'll get lucky."

"Mom's going to be really mad at you," Tycho said.

"Mom's always mad at me," Jessica said. "She's never satisfied no matter what I do."

"Well, you're not nice to her. You talk nice to Daddy, but you're always *nya-nya-nya* with Mom."

"She doesn't like me. She only likes you, Tycho."

"But if you were nice to her —"

"Then she'd boss me around all the time. Do this, do that, make your bed, pick up your clothes. She never just sits quiet and talks to me the way Daddy does."

"Mom doesn't like to talk. She likes to do things."

Jessica looked at him, surprised again by how sharp her little brother was. To show him she still knew more than he did, she said, "Daddy says because Mom was a foster child and nobody loved her she has a hard time with feelings."

"What's a foster child?" Tycho asked.

"It's if your parents can't take care of you."

"Are we going to be foster children now?"

"What do you mean? We've got parents."

"But Daddy —" Tycho began.

"Tycho, please," Jessica begged, wanting to scream. "Please, please, please shut up."

"Okay," he agreed.

They hiked on in silence. It took a while before her mind stopped churning enough that Jessica could notice where they were going. Then she stopped in a clearing and looked back. They'd been climbing steadily, which was good because the state park was basically a valley. Up meant they'd have to arrive in Oldminesville eventually.

"We should see a road soon, Tycho," she said to encourage him.

They didn't though. There was just woods and more woods and then more and more, until Jessica was no longer sure whether they were trudging uphill or downhill. The sound of water drew her toward the right. "We'll find the stream and follow it," she said.

"I don't want to follow anything," Tycho complained. "I want to go home." His eye sockets were smudged with exhaustion and his lips were trembling. If he started crying, she was afraid she'd cry with him.

"You can wash your feet in the stream. That'll make you feel better," she said quickly.

The noise came from layers of rapids in a narrow

brook. Water was arching in rushes of white from stone to stone. Below the steepest drop, the water stilled to fill a wider channel. Tycho took his shoes and socks off, sat down on a mossy fallen tree trunk, and stuck his feet into the cold water. Jessica sat beside him.

Downstream, where the water curved around a bend and disappeared, she was startled to see a boy emerge from under the low-hanging bough of a fir tree. He hadn't seen her. Something furtive about him made her hesitate before calling out to him. "Who's that?" Tycho asked her.

"I don't know," she murmured. Then the boy turned toward her, and she recognized him. "It's Tim," she told Tycho, "from my old school."

Tim looked as skimpy and uncared-for as ever in his tee shirt with the sleeves torn off and his tattered jeans. Dirty too. He used to smell sometimes, she remembered. Jenny, whose mother knew everybody, said Tim lived in a trailer with a whole bunch of brothers and sisters and none of them washed much. But he was carrying a fishing pole and a pail and he must know the way out of here.

"Hi, Tim," Jessica called, hoping the sound of her voice wouldn't scare him off. He scared easily. In school, he'd hang around anyone who would let him during recess, but he'd duck and run if you made a fist at him. Jia Jia hadn't liked him. She'd often made a fist and shouted, "Boo!" so that he wouldn't listen in on their secret conversations.

Tim came a little closer. He was staring, but it took him a long minute to recognize Jessica. He had worn glasses to school for a while, and the teacher had been enthusiastic when he was suddenly able to sound out words in reading, but then he had lost the glasses. He wasn't wearing any now.

"It's Jessica," she said. "From school? We're lost, Tim. We were trying to get back to Oldminesville through the park and we got lost. We've been lost since yesterday."

"It's that way," he said and pointed upstream.

"Is it far?"

He shrugged.

"Well, could you show us? Please, Tim," she begged. She'd had enough of following the sun and not knowing if she was going the right way.

Tycho was hurrying to get his socks and shoes back on.

"I got to get home with this fish I caught," Tim said. As if to emphasize the point, a tail flipped up briefly above the rim of the pail.

"Do you live near the road?"

He shrugged again and glanced into the woods to his right. She was afraid he might take off and leave them any second now.

"We really need help, Tim," she begged.

He hung his head and muttered to himself, shifting the pail from one hand to the other. Once in school she had given him her lunch when she didn't feel like eating it. And sometimes she had given him notepaper and lent him pencils when he sat near her. Not that he asked for anything, but his silent, shameful neediness asked for him.

She hadn't always been nice to him, though. A couple of times she had changed her seat to get away from him, and often she had pretended not to notice that he had nothing to write with.

"Okay, I guess you could follow me," Tim said finally. "My big sister Cora's not there. But when she gets home from work, you better be gone. Cora don't like us to have company."

Was his home another hiding place in the woods? Jessica wondered. "Are you near the road?" she asked him again as Tycho stood up and followed her toward Tim.

"Pretty near. You'll see."

"Well, can I use your phone?"

"We don't have a phone. Cora uses the phone at the diner where she works, like if she has to talk to the school or the government for us."

"I really have to call my mother."

"Cora could do it for you. Maybe. You could give me the number and I'll tell her to call."

"I'd rather do it myself," Jessica said.

"They won't let you."

That didn't make much sense to Jessica, but she didn't bother arguing. The main thing was to get out of the woods. They came to a low wall of boulders and climbed over it. Next they had to weave their way through a dense forest of overgrown Christmas trees whose intertwined branches kept blocking their passage. Tim crouched and continued to move so rapidly that Jessica, who was a head taller than he, had a hard time following him. Even Tycho, who was the smallest, struggled to push branches aside getting through.

"Here we are," Tim said suddenly. He had stopped in a clearing that looked like the back end of a dump. Plastic bags and mounds of assorted bedsprings and junked cars and metal parts were heaped in a semicircle around a trailer that didn't look much better than junk itself. It had once been blue and white, but large patches of rust discolored the painted metal. Two small children were picking burrs out of a dog's matted fur. Chickens strutted around the bare yard, pecking at the ground.

The door of the trailer opened, and out came a girl as skimpy as Tim but maybe a year or two younger. "Did you catch anything?" she asked.

"Yeah, got a trout and some sunnies," Tim said.

"Who're they?" the girl demanded, slitting her eyes meanly at Jessica and Tycho.

"She went to school with me. I'm just gonna show them the road. They got lost in the woods."

"Cora's going to be mad at you."

"What for? I didn't do nothing wrong," Tim said. "You shut your mouth and mind your own business, Lila."

"I have to go to the bathroom," Tycho announced.

"Go in the woods then. You can't use our bathroom," Lila said.

"Oh, Lila, don't be that way. He can use our bathroom. Go ahead," Tim said to Tycho. "You go on in. It's that first door in the hall."

Tycho immediately climbed the cinderblock steps to the trailer door. Lila backed out of sight. Jessica followed her brother in case he needed protection from Lila, whose evil expression made her seem almost as dangerous as Tilda had at first meeting.

Standing outside the closed door of the small bathroom, Jessica looked down the narrow hall into the trailer's living room and kitchen. A wall phone caught her eye. When Tycho came out of the bathroom, accompanied by the sound of the flushing toilet, she pushed him ahead of her back outside.

The two youngest children were chasing the dog around the closest mound of metal scrap. Jessica faced Tim and said accusingly, "You do, too, have a phone."

"Well, but it don't work. Right after my ma left, it stopped working. Cora said she couldn't pay the bill."

"When is your mother coming back?" Jessica asked.

"We don't know," Tim said. "Last time she went away, she was gone a month and we ran out of food and almost had to go tell the County Welfare lady. But now Cora's got a job and she brings us food, and it's summer so we don't have to pay the propane tank man, and the water here's good. There's a well, see."

"But, Tim," Jessica said. "Who takes care of you?"

"Cora does."

"You don't have a father?"

"No, he died a long time ago."

"Our daddy died Friday," Tycho said.

"He did?" Tim seemed impressed. He looked at Jessica with wide-eyed sympathy. "Your daddy died?"

She shook her head vehemently, then stopped and pressed her lips together. Her eyes sought refuge in the bare-branched geranium making a blotch of orange against the dirt area next to the trailer.

"I met your daddy," Tim said. "He was at the party at the church. He asked me what grade I was in, and then he said you was in my grade so I deserved an extra prize. It was a girl's toy, though. I gave it to Lila. It was beads you string to make a bracelet. Lila liked it pretty good."

Jessica nodded. She couldn't remember Daddy helping with any church party recently, but he was always helping somebody in town — lending them a hand to move something or getting their sick grandparent to swallow medicine or taking people to the doctor's. She hadn't tried to keep track of where he went. So long as he was there for her when he got back, she had been satisfied.

"He's a big guy, isn't he?" Tim said with admiration. "Bet they needed a really long coffin for him."

"He wasn't in a coffin," Jessica shouted in a sudden rage. "He didn't die. He went home to the grandparents' house. That's where he is and I'm *not* crazy."

"Yes, she is," Tycho said.

Tim gave them both time to calm down. Then he said, "It's a long way from here to your house. You should go up to the road and see if somebody'll give you a ride maybe."

"Where *is* the road?" Jessica demanded impatiently.

"You go through the dump that way" — he pointed — "and you'll see a dirt road. Follow it to the entrance, and then you go that way toward Oldminesville." He gestured vigorously to the right. She remembered a student teacher last year trying to teach Tim his left from his right by writing on the back of his hand with magic marker. Kids had made fun of him about it at recess.

"Thanks," Jessica said.

"You want to give me that number for Cora to call?"

"I don't have anything to write it on," Jessica said.

"Here." Tim carefully tore a corner out of the scribbled page of a coloring book lying on the top step of the trailer. Jessica wrote the numbers small and neat with the red crayon he handed her. Gravely he pocketed the scrap of paper.

"When will she get home?" Jessica asked.

"Soon. She usually comes on her lunch hour to check on us. See, the twins are always getting in trouble. Lila's supposed to watch them, but she don't."

"Couldn't you watch them?" Jessica asked.

"Yeah, I do when I'm around. But like I got work to do, too, you know."

The idea that children could survive without parents to care for them was new to Jessica, and she was filled with respect for Tim that he could do it. "Well, thanks," she said. "I guess we'd better go. Don't forget to give your sister the number. Okay?"

"Okay." He nodded without disturbing the slight frown that was his usual expression.

Tycho was pulling at a wheel sticking out of the pile of rubbish on the side of the yard. "Come on, Tycho." She took his arm.

"But this would be a good wheel to make a go-cart, Jessica."

"No," she hissed at him. "It doesn't belong to us. Come on now."

He frowned at her resentfully, but he came. He was getting more and more stubborn, she thought, as she steered them through the dump toward the road. He used to agree to anything she said and cooperate without giving her any grief. Now he had his own ideas. She thought of Lila, who was supposed to be in charge of those wild little kids. And how did Cora, the oldest sister, take care of them all without a mother or father to help? It wasn't fair for a girl to have to carry that much responsibility, even if she was the oldest.

Jessica was more tired than she'd ever been in her life. Mom, she thought with relief as she spotted the asphalt of the highway at last. One phone call from any neighbor's house would bring Mom, ready and willing to take charge of both her children.

But now that they had managed to get to Oldminesville, the phone call could wait a little while longer, at
least until Jessica had the satisfaction of showing Tycho
that she wasn't crazy. She did know their father best,
and soon she'd prove it.

Chapter Nine

The minute Jessica spotted the empty booth where the man usually sat to check on dump stickers, she knew where she was. Daddy had taken her with him on the five-minute drive to the dump often enough. She set off down the dirt road to the highway, hoping some neighbor would pass and give Tycho and her a ride. The grandparents' house was a couple of miles farther on the highway, just before the all-purpose country store–gas station–post office, which was the center of Oldminesville.

Tycho slogged along beside her complaining about being hungry again. "Why didn't you ask that kid for something to eat?" he grumbled.

"Because they're poor, Tycho. They probably don't have that much to eat themselves."

"Well, they had a well," he said. "We could have had water."

"We'll get a drink when we get to the grandparents' house. And I can call Mom from there."

"Tim said he'd make his sister call."

"Yes, but he said she doesn't like people coming to their place, so she might not want to call Mom for us. Anyway, Tim might forget."

"He won't forget. He was nice."

"He is nice," Jessica agreed, although his niceness was a new discovery for her. "I never heard him talk so much before. In school he's shy."

"Anyway, I wouldn't like to live where they live," Tycho said.

"Me neither."

"And he doesn't have a daddy."

"And his mother just went off and left them to take care of themselves." Jessica shook her head in disbelief that an adult could be so irresponsible.

"Our mother wouldn't do that, would she, Jessica?"

"Of course not." It comforted Jessica to think that however bossy and unappreciative Mom was, she could be relied on to take care of them.

"Yeah." Tycho suddenly inserted his hand into Jessica's and walked more confidently. "Anyway, that Lila's too little to be watching the other kids."

"Too mean, too," Jessica said.

She took a deep breath. It was tiring to be the big sister continuously. Right now she'd be glad if her parents suddenly showed up to take over for her. "Get in the car, kids. We were worried about you," they'd say. And then she and Tycho would hop in the back seat. Free of the burden of planning and solving their own problems, they could spill out the story of their adventures, while their parents listened and marveled at how well they had managed by themselves in the woods.

Tycho started waving vigorously at a pickup truck coming toward them. Mrs. Burns, who ran the country store, was the driver. She lifted her hand from the steering wheel and waved without slowing down, as if seeing them on the road was to be expected.

In dismay, Jessica looked over her shoulder at the bushy tail of dust left by the truck, which was loaded with lumpy plastic garbage bags. "She must have forgotten we moved," Jessica said.

"Anyway, she's going the wrong way," Tycho pointed out.

He yawned and Jessica felt guilty. They still had a hike ahead of them, past empty fields and the big barn where auctions were held on summer weekends, past woodlots and the old quarry that wasn't used anymore.

They would cross the road where Jia Jia lived, in the house next door to the little white steepled church where her father was the minister, but Jessica didn't feel like stopping to visit her friend. Besides, Jia Jia was probably at day camp. And Jenny, who also lived in a house down that road, would be off in the family's camp trailer to visit her relatives. But that didn't matter because Jessica didn't feel like seeing her, either.

"How are we going to get into the house?" Tycho asked. "Do you have the key?"

"Oh no!" she said. "I saved it, but I forgot to bring it."

"We could go to Mr. Jessup's house and call Mom."

It struck Jessica that this wasn't the first time on the trip that Tycho had pointed something out to her. He was practical, more practical than she was anyway. She considered making a detour to Mr. Jessup's hosue. He was their nearest neighbor, but he was ancient and he could neither see nor hear well. "Let's see if we can't get into the kitchen first," she said. "The lock's still broken on that window."

"Mom told Dad he had to fix it for the people that bought the house."

"I know, but he didn't. He took me out to see the apple blossoms instead and then something else happened. I don't remember what."

"Why didn't you ask me to go see the apple blossoms, too, Jessica?"

"Because you don't care about things like that, Tycho."

"You and Daddy always do stuff and you never take me," Tycho complained quietly.

"Yes, we do too take you. Lots of times we take you. . . . Anyway, I was Daddy's child long before you were born. We always did things together, just him and me. Even Mom didn't go."

"Mom does things with *both* you and me."

"Not fun things. Daddy's the one who does fun things. Mom just takes us to get haircuts or to the doctor."

Mom wanted adult company when she got home after being in school with kids all day. Or anyway, that's what Jessica had heard her say when friends called to invite her to something. "Sure, if we can get a baby sitter, we'll come. I need some grown-up conversation," Mom would tell her caller.

But Daddy never said he needed adults. Daddy was happy doing quiet things with his kids, even if it was just looking at a barn swallow feeding its babies, or playing a board game. Still, it was mean to pick out all Mom's faults. The truth was she was a pretty good parent. It wasn't her fault that she wasn't as lovable as Daddy. After all, who was? In her heart Jessica knew she could never measure up to Daddy, either.

She made a face at the blue jay who was squawking from a branch over their heads to warn them out of his territory.

"Jessica —" Tycho began with such caution that she knew what was coming.

"Oh, be quiet," she said to shut him up before he tried to make her know what she wasn't ready to know yet.

"We're almost there now, and you can get yourself a drink of water at our own kitchen sink."

The grandparents' house was on a hillside off the highway and up a curved dirt driveway. It was tall and white with a steep green roof outlined by curly, dark green trim that also edged the front porch overhang. To Jessica, the grandparents' house looked much prettier than the plain white copycat split-level in the new development in Hammond. She couldn't imagine why Mom liked the split-level better.

"Why are you letting her make us move?" Jessica had asked Daddy.

"Your mother has a right to have something she wants now and then," he'd said. "I promised her when I married her I'd make her happy. She's not very happy in Oldminesville, Jessica."

Way off to the left behind the fallen-down barn was the climbing tree, and way off to the right on the hill higher than the house was the old apple orchard. The garage and storage shed came first on the curving driveway. Next came the lilac bushes that were still full of fragrant purple blooms.

"*Here's* my water pistol," Tycho said. He plucked the green plastic gun from the grass. The grass needed cutting again, although Daddy had mowed it just before the move.

Jessica stood on the back steps of the house and reached over to lift up the kitchen window the way

Daddy often had. He regularly forgot his key because he hadn't needed it before he married Mom, when the house was never locked. Mom believed in locks. She had grown up in a city where it was either lock the doors or get robbed. Jessica struggled to budge the window and failed. Daddy had long arms.

"I'll get the ladder," Tycho said. He went for the short old wooden one they'd left in the garage for the new owners who were going to move in sometime this summer. His tiredness seemed to be forgotten now that they'd arrived.

The ladder made it possible to open the window. Jessica climbed onto the sill and dropped to the old-fashioned red brick vinyl floor. Dad had wanted to have the same pattern in the new house. "No way, pal," Mom had said. "I always hated that red brick."

"You never told me that!" Daddy had said.

"Well, it belonged with the house," Mom had said.

Jessica opened the back door from the inside. Then she shut the window in case she forgot and left it open for the rain to come in. Stripped of table and chairs and refrigerator, the kitchen looked naked.

Tycho turned on the faucet in the sink, but there were no glasses in the cupboard. Everything had been packed. Jessica dug the used cups out of the backpack for yet another time. After they had filled themselves up on the cold well water, she went purposefully to the kitchen wall phone. Mom hadn't packed it because it was

105

cracked on one side. No dial tone. Hadn't they paid their bill?

"I guess we can't use it," Jessica said. "I guess it's been disconnected."

"We could go to Mr. Jessup's," Tycho said, looking warily around the bare kitchen.

"Probably Tim's sister will call," Jessica reasoned. Going to Mr. Jessup's house would be such an effort, and she felt strangely drained of energy.

The grandparents' house seemed eerily different. To reassure herself she said, "Daddy always sat at that end of the table — when the table was there — so he could stretch his legs out. Do you remember how you rode his legs when you were little, Tycho? You used to grab him round the knees, and he'd buck you up, and you'd laugh so hard that you'd make Mom and me laugh with you."

"Yes, I remember."

She didn't think he did, but she didn't challenge him. "Mom always tells Daddy to sit up straight. She says slumping in a chair like Daddy does gives you a bad back. I slump sometimes, too."

"No, you don't," Tycho said. "You sit up straight just like Mom."

Did she? Jessica didn't bother to argue. Instead, she led the way to the living room through the little hall lined with emptied pantry shelves. The living room shocked her. On the walls were ghostly spaces where pictures had hung, and the scratches on the wooden floor glared where there hadn't been any rugs. There was the deep gouge that Jessica had made dragging the metal plant stand that Mom had forbidden her to touch. "Now how are we going to punish you?" Daddy had asked sorrowfully.

"I don't know!" Jessica had cried, young enough then to image that a really terrible punishment awaited her.

"I think you had better write your mother a letter and tell her how sorry you are you disobeyed her. Meanwhile I'll see what I can do to fix the floor," Daddy had said.

He hadn't been able to fix it very well, although he'd filled and stained the gouge. As for the letter, it had taken Jessica forever to write because she'd only been in first grade and had to ask Daddy to spell most of the words for her.

Mom had finally covered the gouge by moving the rug into the center of the room, even though it looked odd there. Now, with the floor bare, the evidence of Jessica's old misdeed was plain to see. It made her glad to think that the people who had bought the house would never get it out. It meant that something of her would stay here forever.

June sunshine was cascading through the uncurtained window, but the woodsy odor from winter fires in the fireplace still hung in the room. "Remember last fall when it rained and we couldn't go camping and Daddy got us branches and we toasted marshmallows in the fireplace and he told us stories?" Jessica asked Tycho.

"What stories?" Tycho asked. He aimed his green squirtgun at the window and made shooting noises.

"Like the one about the cookie monster who got so fat from eating cookies that he couldn't get out of his house, and so a little girl came and played with him and he was glad to have a friend, and so he shared his cookies with her and then he got thin again. You remember, Tycho."

"Oh, yeah. And about Bigfoot."

"Daddy has the biggest feet," Jessica said vaguely. She couldn't recall any Bigfoot story her father had ever told them. Could she have forgotten? The question gave her such a pang she decided that most likely Daddy had told Tycho the story when she wasn't there.

"Am I going to have big feet, Jessica?"

"No, you're small like Mom. I got the big feet. I hope they don't get too big, though." She looked down at her sneakers. In gym when her sneakers were lined up with the other kids, they stuck out by inches. It made them easier to identify, but big feet were ugly on a girl.

Tycho was at the front door turning the handle so he could get out. Jessica wasn't ready to leave. She might never be ready to leave here again. Trying to keep him with her, she said, "Tycho, remember the night of the thunderstorm?"

"No." He gave up trying to unlock the front door and went to the half door under the stairs where they'd stored things like suitcases and toys. That door was easy to open. Bending way over, he peered around inside the dark space where they had often hidden when they played hide-and-go-seek.

"You do so remember," Jessica insisted. "You and I both woke up. That thunder was awful, and you were crying, and Daddy came upstairs and carried us down to the living room, and he and Mom had a blanket, and we all got under the blanket together like it was a tent. And then Daddy tickled Mom and she giggled, and we were all giggling and rolling on the couch under the blanket, and you got mad and said, 'Stop this now!' You were only two, and everybody thought you were so funny that we all laughed more and more until the thunder stopped."

"I don't remember," Tycho said stubbornly. "Let me out now, Jessica. Please?"

In silence she unlocked the double lock on the front door for him. "I'll come out in a while," she said.

She watched her little brother stroll toward the garage. Next to it was the enormous sandbox that Daddy had built for them. It still held a few rusty construction toys that Tycho had abandoned. "Daddy," Jessica called softly. "Daddy, where are you?"

She moved into the torrent of sunshine and closed her eyes, hoping for magic. But when she opened her eyes, the room was still achingly empty, so empty it seemed impossible it would ever be filled again. The people who had bought the house were an older couple without children, Mom had said. Even if they'd paid for it, they had no right to live here. Nobody but her family should live in this house that the grandparents had built.

Daddy had grown up here. He had sat in the old leather armchair that Mom had made him throw out when they moved to Hammond. And he'd stretched out his legs on the hassock and listened to Jessica explaining how rotten and unfair the teacher had been, or about what her friend had done to her on the bus, or about how Mom liked Tycho better than Jessica.

"Never mind, baby," he'd say in his deep voice that vibrated like a cat purring. "Tomorrow will go better. It'll come out all right, you'll see."

"Why should it, Daddy?"

"Because you're an exceptionally terrific kid," he'd say. And sometimes he'd add that she was beautiful and always he'd tell her how much he loved her. Then she'd burrow into his chest, assured by the strength of his arms around her that everything was all right.

The hollow silence in this house that had always been full of friendly hums and creaks began to drag on Jessica's spirits. She considered checking out the bedrooms, but she didn't have the energy to climb the stairs. Instead, she followed Tycho outside to the sandbox where he was standing listlessly with a shovel in his hand.

"I wish Mom would come," Tycho said without looking around to check who was behind him. "You said Daddy was going to be here, but he's not."

"Yes, he is."

"No, he's not. Daddy's dead. He got killed by a car. I *wish* you wouldn't act like you don't know that, Jessica. It scares me."

A coldness clamped down in Jessica's chest. "Even if he did get killed, he's here," she heard herself say stubbornly.

Her own words made her shiver. Desperate to take back the admission she'd accidentally made, she veered away from it, asking Tycho, "Because where else would he be?" Hadn't Daddy's friend said Daddy would be with her? He was a priest and he should know, shouldn't he? Daddy loved her too much to go very far away.

"You know what makes me mad," she said with her heart beating wildly. "What makes me mad is that they didn't even care."

"Who didn't?"

"The stupid people who came. The uncles didn't even talk about Daddy. They just talked about how their car broke down and made them miss the service. And those were his *brothers*. Like all they cared about was being late. And everybody else was being sorry for Mom, like something terrible had happened to *her*. But she was fine. It was Daddy who —"

Tycho looked at her, waiting for her to say it.

But she couldn't yet. "I'm going down to the climbing tree," she said. "Want to come with me?"

"Aren't you going to call Mom?"

"Maybe he died," Jessica said furiously. "But nobody

acted right about it. They talked like they didn't even know who he was." Tycho looked up at her with a puzzled frown.

In disgust she turned around and marched across the backyard toward the other end of the property where the climbing tree was reaching heavenward. She was so angry she wanted to kick something, so angry she hated the whole world, so angry she was afraid she was going to blaze up like a faulty rocket and smash to earth and die.

Well, so what if she did die. She didn't care. Not if Daddy wasn't around anymore.

Chapter Ten

The climbing tree was unlike any other tree in the valley. Taller than most houses, its arms stretched out so far on every side of its lumpy, misshapen trunk that it could have sheltered everyone in Oldminesville.

The solitary giant beech stood at the back of an overgrown pasture studded with hummocks of grass and great flat rocks furry with lichen. Thistles and milk-weeds and mullein grew in the field now, where thirty years ago cows had grazed. Jessica raced for the tree, Daddy's tree, as if she could outrun the pain, as if the tree would cure it.

"Jessica, Jessica, wait for me!" Tycho called after her, but she didn't stop until she got to the piled-up rocks that used to support the barbed wire fence around the old cow pasture. There she halted.

Here was the pet cemetery. Scattered rocks and stick crosses marked the graves. The fallen sticks nearest the rock wall were for the grandmother's two white cats; they had still been alive when Jessica was Tycho's age. Daddy's dog, Goofer, was buried under a slab that said, "Good dog, Goofer." Even chipmunks and mice had markers for their graves. So did the rabbit, the one that Jessica and Daddy had kept alive for a month after the cat got it.

The newest grave was Mimsy's. Jessica had painted her cat's name on the rock there herself a week ago when she had thought losing her cat was the worst thing that could ever happen to her.

And where was Daddy's grave? If he was dead, if his warm arms would never hug her again, where could she go to be near him? Cremated. The idea of burning up a person was so hideous! To put big-teddy-bear-sweet Daddy into a fire and destroy even his bones so that nothing was left of him but ashes was a more terrible act than Jessica could imagine.

A twisting pain turned her away from the pet grave-yard. But before she took another step toward the climbing tree, Tycho caught up with her. "You're mean," he said. "Why didn't you wait for me, Jessica?"

She didn't answer him. She licked her dry lips and closed her eyes.

"Jessica?" he said, as he noticed where they were. "Is Mimsy a skeleton yet?"

She sucked in her breath, opened her eyes, and answered him. "I don't know."

"Daddy's dead. Is he going to be a skeleton?"

"No."

"But he's dead. So where is his body?"

"Shut *up*, Tycho. Stop talking about it or I'll hit you."
She raised her hand in a frenzy, ready to strike.

He backed off a step. but when she didn't move, he
gained courage and said, "You wouldn't hit me. . . . You
pinch, though." He touched the soft part of his arm as if
he could still feel the hurt from weeks ago.

"Yes, because you deserve it." But she bit her lip,
ashamed of herself. Tycho's just trying to understand,
Daddy would say; he's little. But how could she tell her
brother what she didn't understand herself?

"Let's go to Mr. Jessup's and call Mom now," Tycho
said.

"I have to go to the climbing tree first."

He let out a big sigh as if she were trying his patience.
"Well, don't go so fast then. Okay?"

She didn't want him with her, but with no one else
there to take care of him, she couldn't chase him away.
"Hurry up," she said and set off.

Daddy's name was on the tree; so was his father's.
The tree had grown enough since Jessica's grandfather
had carved his name in block letters into the muscular
trunk that his name was higher up than anyone could
reach from the ground. Below it was a heart Daddy had
carved with his and his first girlfriend's initials.

Farther down and to the right, the year that Tycho
was born, Daddy had carved another heart that said,
"Dad & Jessica." He had carved it for her then because

their whole house seemed to revolve around Tycho, and Jessica had felt as if she didn't matter to anyone anymore.

She cupped her hands around that heart and stared at the dark scar the letters made in the smooth gray bark, remembering Daddy's answer when she'd asked him why he didn't climb the tree anymore. "I've gotten too old for tree climbing," he had said.

"But you're strong, Daddy. You should climb better now you're old."

"Maybe, but a man can't climb a tree and dream out over the world the way a boy can, Jessica."

"Why not?"

"Because what would you think of a grown man standing in a treetop without a saw in his hand or anything practical to show he had a purpose up there?"

"I don't know."

"Most people would think he was crazy," Daddy had said. "And folks around here already doubt my sanity because I became a nurse instead of a doctor."

He had grinned, and she'd thought he might be joking, but she asked him seriously, "Why didn't you become a doctor?"

"Oh, I don't know. Mostly because doctors don't have much time to comfort patients, and comforting is what I'm best at."

The answer had satisfied her so well that she had been surprised when he asked her, "Would you like your daddy to be a doctor, Jessica?"

"No. I like the way you are."

He'd laughed then and hugged her as if she'd pleased him. It didn't take much for her to please him. Just being herself was enough.

"What was it like when you were in the top of the tree?" she had asked.

"Like I was king of the valley," he'd said. "Up there I felt wise. Up there even the big questions had an answer, or one I could imagine anyway."

"Did you feel like a bird?"

"Like an eagle at least." Then he'd smiled his joy-kindling smile and asked if she'd like to climb his tree.

"Oh, yes! Can you take me to the top with you?"

"The top?" He had to lean his head so far back to see it that his neck arched like a bridge. "Well, if you don't get scared, I might get you partway up. . . . Maybe."

It had been the biggest thrill of her life. He had gotten a rope and tied one end around her and one end around his own waist. First, she had followed him up the vertical row of crossbars nailed to the trunk. The ladder stopped at the fat lower branches, which were as thick around as Daddy's chest.

Jessica had already climbed that far alone. This time he'd hoisted her by the arms while she walked her feet up the trunk to the next highest branch. Standing beside him that high up, she was afraid to look down. The tree branches that came next were easy to get to because she could put her foot in a rotted-out cavity in the trunk where a limb had broken off.

117

"High enough?" Daddy had asked her when they reached the branch above the cavity.

She had glanced down to check and grabbed hold of him in terror.

"Don't look down. Look out that way," he'd told her, holding her securely.

Out that way was the lumpy green mattress of tree-tops, sagging in the middle, that was the state park, and beyond that, the small gray blocks that were the city of Hammond, and even farther off was the wavy line of distant mountains.

"What can you see if you go higher, Daddy?"

"The sky, the reach of the world."

"Take me higher then," she had said.

He'd laughed. "When your mother hears about this, she'll get mad at me."

"No, she won't. Anyway, you can always talk her out of being mad."

"I don't think I've ever succeeded in talking her out of anything," he said. "Your mother is one strong-minded lady — like you, Jessica."

They had had the whole afternoon together because Tycho was at a party and Mom was at the mall shopping for clothes. That had been the afternoon when she had bought the flowery cotton dress for Jessica, just a few short weeks ago.

Next Dad had given Jessica a climbing lesson. He had grasped the smooth bark of the trunk with his legs and reached up with one arm for a higher branch and down with the other to help her.

"Don't think about falling," he'd told her. "Thinking about it will just make you shaky. Concentrate on figuring the safest way up. And be sure you test any branch before you give your whole weight to it because it could be rotten and break on you."

"Is this as high as you went when you were a boy?" she had asked him when he said they had climbed enough.

"I don't know if I ever even *made* it this high," he'd said. "You're a real daredevil, Jessica."

She had been proud of herself, standing on a limb there high above the world, and safe as well, with her back against her father and his right arm like a seat belt around her while his left arm clamped them to the trunk. Remember this moment, she had told herself. It had been so special — that heady sense of being cradled in the arms of the tree, rocked by the wind, high above the world and yet secure in her father's arms.

"How come my name's not there where yours is?" Tycho asked.

Jessica dropped her hands from the heart carved in the tree trunk. "Because Daddy carved it when you were just born."

Tycho's mouth turned down. "That's not fair."

"Yes, it's fair."

"No, it's not. He's my daddy, too, you know."

"Tycho, don't be a pain." What a bother he was. She wished he'd go away, but he wasn't budging and his mouth still had its stubborn turtle set. Ignoring him, she eyed the distance between the first easy branch and the next one up. Without Daddy's help, she wasn't likely to get very far.

"Jessica, you've got the knife," Tycho said.

"What?"

"In the backpack."

She touched the straps over her arms, surprised to find she was still wearing the nearly empty pack. "What do you want from me, Tycho?"

"You could put my name with yours."

She hesitated, tempted to refuse and get on with what she meant to do, but she felt her father's eyes on her. He'd have the little smile that meant he was expecting her to do the right thing.

"Okay, okay. I'll carve it, Tycho."

"When?"

"Now."

Resigned, she took out the knife and let the pack drop to the ground. It took a while to cut Tycho's name in next to hers. The letters ran out of the heart, and then she had to make a second heart, joined to the first, to encircle all three names at once. "There," she said, "satisfied?"

He nodded. "I wish Dad was here."

"He's here if he's anywhere."

"But I don't see him, Jessica."

Unshed tears filled her chest and burned her eyes. "You wait for me now. I'm going to climb up," she said.

"Can I come?"

"I'm not strong enough to get both of us up." She said it kindly, the way Daddy would.

Tycho stared at her. Then as if he understood what this meant to her, he said, "Okay, I'll wait."

Up the ladder she went to the first branch, which was too heavy for even the strongest wind to budge. She remembered being a little scared sitting on it when she'd climbed that far alone, even though it was as wide as a chair bottom and she could lean back against the trunk for support. She reached for the notch where the next higher branch joined the trunk and braced her arms on it up to her elbows. That didn't work, though, until she took hold of a knob beyond the notch and pulled herself up.

Her knee reached the limb and she balanced there for a dizzy second. Then she stepped up on the edge of the cavity and grabbed the branch above her. But when she tried to shimmy up the tree, using her knees to hold the trunk and both arms to raise herself, she couldn't do it. The insides of her legs were scraped raw. Nevertheless, she made it to a sitting position at a dizzy height above the ground.

There she gave her trembling muscles a rest and took stock of where she was. A truck on the highway through Oldminesville was the size of one of Tycho's sandbox toys. She hadn't even gotten halfway up the tree, but she could see the whole valley. A jet trailed a white chalk line across the sky. The heads of giant clouds were piling up over Hammond and the mountains beyond it.

Jessica took deep breaths. How could it be in this world where trucks still droned along the highway, and clouds piled up to threaten rain, and the sun went down after dinner and rose before breakfast, that Daddy could disappear? Daddy was as steady as the sun, as solid as the truck. He belonged in her life as surely as the earth under her feet. For him to be gone was just not possible.

"Jessica!" Tycho called sharply.

"What?" His anxious face looking up at her was doll-sized.

"Come down now. Okay?"

"Not yet. I'm not done climbing." She hadn't known she had to go higher until she said it. Now she began figuring the next step up. It seemed there were more branches to choose from, and they were smaller around. And with the trunk of the tree thinner this high off the ground, she could grip it more easily with her legs when she had to.

She felt the ache in her arms as soon as she let them take her weight.

There was no need to save strength for her descent because she just might not go down. She just might decide to stay up here, be an eagle, be lord of the world with Daddy.

A pain ripped through her. "Daddy," she whispered. "Daddy." And the sweat came out on her forehead and her arms ached, and she felt as if she were being shredded.

"Jessica!" Tycho screamed. "Jessica, come *downnnnn*!"

She closed her eyes, swaying with the upper branches. Wind was wheezing round her now and shushing her. Leaves tickled her face. When she looked out over the valley, she seemed to be at eye level with the ghostly humps of the mountains in the west. The clouds had parted and the sun shone right in her eyes so she couldn't look in that direction for long.

A shadow swiftly darkened the clotted green of the state forest. The big clouds were coming closer, and the wind was picking up. What if a storm came? She could die if the wind tore her from the tree and she fell from this height. She could die easily if she fell, as easily as Daddy had been killed on the highway when he went out for ice cream. Death could happen very easily, she knew. Mimsy had died. Daddy had died. Did it matter if she did, too?

"Jessica, Jessica, you've got to come *downnnnnnn*!"

Her eyes went to her frantic brother and sudden fear made her feel nauseated. "Daddy?" She didn't expect him to answer anymore. Wherever he was, he couldn't come when she called him no matter how she begged.

"Daddy," she whispered sorrowfully. The impossible, the unendurable, had really happened. He was ashes now, not even a body in a box in the ground, but ashes — as if he were nothing.

"Daddy," she pleaded. "I can't do this without you." And she screamed, screamed in fury that such a thing could happen to her.

"Jessica, you're scaring me," Tycho yelled. "Please, come down. Please. I need you."

She breathed deeply, swaying with the rushing wind, which was so strong now that she was swinging, tangled arms and legs clinging to the thin branches, leaves slapping lightly against her skin. The tree itself seemed to wail around her in a shushing, hissing chorus. She closed her eyes and let herself be carried with the wind's force. And then it stilled, and she was still clinging to her cradle of branches.

Below her Tycho was sobbing now. He needed her. She was the big sister, and what was she doing up in this treetop? She had to get down. Except she couldn't move. Fear had frozen her.

"I can't do it, Tycho," she called down to him. "You better go to Mr. Jessup's and call Mom."

Immediately he stopped crying. He swiped at his face with his arm and trotted off fast. Overcome with tiredness, Jessica closed her eyes. Concentrate, she told herself. Hold tight to these branches. And stay alive.

Chapter Eleven

It didn't take long for Jessica to get dizzy in her treetop swing. To keep herself still — which was to keep herself safe — she sang the old nursery lullaby that fit her predicament all too well, except that she was no baby. "Rock-a-bye baby, in the tree top, when the wind blows the cradle will rock. . . ."

Little balloons of fear blew up in her chest. She worked at deflating them by figuring out how much time it would take Tycho to get to Mr. Jessup's house and make the old man understand that she was in trouble. Half an hour? And then Mr. Jessup would have to find the new phone number in Hammond because Tycho didn't know it yet. And then more time would be needed for Mom to drive here.

Jessica had herself convinced that she would need to cling to her treetop cradle for another hour at least when she saw three dark heads hurrying toward her. They looked like a family — not her family because she and Daddy were big and blond. But Mom and Tycho were slight and dark-haired, and so was Alan.

It made Jessica feel strange to see Alan there with her mother and brother, as if he were trying to take Daddy's place. Not that Alan could, ever. He wasn't as strong or as kind as Daddy. The smile on his long narrow face wasn't warming the way Daddy's smile was. Alan was a good guy, but no more than Daddy's shadow.

"Jessica!" Mom's hands went to her cheeks in terror and her face grew distorted with fear when she saw how high up her daughter had climbed. "What are you doing up there? Do you want to get killed?"

Alan had stopped behind Mom. Now he put his hand over her mouth and said, "Hush. You'll upset her."

"I'm okay," Jessica said in a loud, calm voice to settle Mom down.

Impatiently, Mom pushed Alan's hand away from her face. Good, Jessica thought.

"Just don't move, darling." Mom held her palm out in a stop sign as if Jessica might be planning to leap down from her perch. "We'll get the fire department. They'll help you down."

"The fire department? I'm not a cat," Jessica said scornfully. Her fear had shrunk to a small hard nugget, which she could ignore now that she wasn't alone anymore. Warily, she surveyed the branches under her. "I can get down by myself," she announced.

Their anxious faces somehow gave her confidence. Hadn't Daddy called her a daredevil? Her first move was the hardest. She had to make herself let go with her right arm, which was anchoring her to the tree trunk, take hold of a thinner branch, and let her feet down in order to reach a thick branch just a few feet beneath her. There. She hugged the trunk again with both arms and eased herself down it to a sitting position.

Going down was much more difficult than climbing up had been because now Jessica was aware that she might slip and fall. Still holding the trunk, she turned onto her stomach and began feeling with her feet for the branch below her and to the right.

"Don't, Jessica!" Alan called. "It's too dangerous. Wait till I get a ladder, at least."

"We don't got one tall enough," Tycho said. His lapse into babyish speech made Jessica seek his face. He looked fearful, fearful for her. She remembered how fine he'd been in the woods and how well he'd dealt with Tilda. He was turning from a helpless baby who depended on her for everything into a real companion.

Mom put her arms around Tycho and he leaned his head back against her stomach, peering up at Jessica worriedly. Jessica smiled at him, feeling warm with love for him.

"Jessica, please. What if you fall and hurt yourself?" Mom sounded close to tears. "I couldn't bear it. *Please* stay put until we get help."

"Daddy taught me to climb," Jessica said. "Don't worry, Mom." She wanted to do it alone. Now that Daddy was gone, she would have to do a lot of things alone. She studied the next set of branches raying out beneath her. This time she slid her right foot down, bending the knee of her left leg almost to her chin until the tip of her toe touched the branch she wanted. She let her other limbs down one by one.

When she was only house-high above the ground, she stopped to rest. As soon as she did, her muscles began trembling, and the rubbed-raw places on her hands and the insides of her legs stung.

"Jessica —" Mom began.

"How did you get here so fast anyway?" Jessica asked to distract her mother and give herself time to rest.

"We found Tycho on the road. He was heading toward Mr. Jessup's house and we were coming here," Mom said. "Alan guessed where you might be."

Alan? How would he know where she'd go? Jessica glanced at his tense face and turned quickly away. She asked her mother, "Did Tim's sister call you?"

"Who's Tim?" Mom asked.

"He lives in a trailer," Tycho said. "He showed us the way out of the woods."

"Were you in the woods all last night?" Mom sounded alarmed. She looked so hollow-eyed that Jessica felt sorry for her. "It was okay, Mom," she said. "We slept in an old lady's house."

"But why didn't she call me? Jessica, why didn't *you* call me? How could you do such a thing? I was worried half out of my mind."

Guiltily Jessica explained, "Well, Tilda didn't have a phone, and —" She stopped herself before saying anything that would give Tilda away.

"But to run away from home like that? How could you do such a thing when your father — how could you, Jessica?" Mom's hands writhed and her face twisted as if someone were wringing out her skin.

"We didn't mean to get lost," Tycho offered.

"I *didn't* run away from home with Tycho, Mom." Jessica was indignant that her mother could think she would be that childish. "I just needed to come here, and I thought if we cut through the woods it wouldn't be far."

"But you left without telling me where you were going."

"I figured it wouldn't take long. I didn't know the woods went on forever. And we got lost. It wasn't fun. We had to walk and walk and — It wasn't fun at all. But we *did* try to find a telephone. We really did."

"I called Jia Jia and Jenny," Mom said. "And the police. They're probably out looking for you now. They told me to stay home in case you called, but then when Alan thought you might be here —"

"Because I know what this place means to you," Alan put in.

Jessica stared at him. When had he learned to understand her so well? He had never paid that much attention to her. Daddy was the one he came to talk to — or Mom. It was only when both adults were busy, or when Alan babysat as a favor to them, that he talked to Jessica and Tycho at all. "I wanted to find Daddy," she muttered.

"Jessica," Mom said in a strangled voice. "He's dead."

"I know that," Jessica said with a sad acceptance that was, at least, more tolerable than the fierce denial that had driven her to climb the tree.

For some reason her answer made Mom sob. She laid her cheek on Tycho's head and held on to him while she wept. Tycho never took his eyes off Jessica. In a voice sad as a mourning dove's, he begged, "Please, come down, Jessica."

She was weary and every part of her ached as she set herself to easing onto the next layer of tree limbs. When she reached the notch where the big branch had rotted out, she rested again.

Mom was standing up, wiping her tears and watching her more calmly. No doubt she expected that once Jessica got herself down from the tree everything would be normal again. Mom being Mom, that's how she would want it. They'd go back to the house in Hammond and Mom would remind Jessica to set the table for dinner and tonight they'd watch television.

"You'd better call Jenny and Jia Jia and tell them

you're all right," Mom would say, and Jessica would call and maybe Jia Jia would promise to spend next weekend with her. Everything so normal and regular that it would smooth over Daddy's place in their lives as if he had never been. But Jessica wouldn't allow that. Daddy couldn't disappear from her life, ever. Not even turning him to ashes could make him disappear. Her fingers tightened on the branch she was gripping.

"You didn't even bury him the right way," she accused her mother.

Mom flinched as if she'd been slapped. "I did what he wanted."

"But you don't know what he wanted. He never expected to get killed, not really."

"Jessica," Mom's voice was shaky as she said, "believe me. I loved your father. It hurts me when you act as if I didn't. Why are you blaming me? It's not my fault he's not here anymore."

"Because," Jessica said. She didn't know why. Because Daddy's dying had to be somebody's fault. It could be God was to blame. But God was the shepherd. And why would God let a man like Daddy, who did so much good in the world, die young? God had to know how important Daddy was.

"Jessica," Mom said. "I know this is terrible for you. But believe me, it's terrible for me, too. What we have to do is make this bring us closer together. You and Tycho and I are the only family we have left."

Jessica shook her head. Quietly she said, "It's you and Tycho. Like it was Daddy and me. You even said so, Mom. You said I was Daddy's girl."

"Don't you have any idea how much I love you?" Mom asked. She spoke slowly to emphasize her words. "You are my daughter, my first child. And you're so like your father. And I don't *have* him anymore. Oh, my God!" She put her fist to her mouth to stifle her sob.

Jessica glanced at Alan, who was watching her with amazement. Did her mother love her that much? Had she been wrong about that, too? She took a deep breath, and under the stricken eyes of her mother and brother, she descended the rest of the way. Immediately, she went to her mother and embraced her, dropping her head onto her mother's shoulder as Tycho wriggled away.

"Mom, Jessica put my name in with hers and Daddy's," Tycho said. "See there on the tree?"

"That's nice," Mom murmured.

"Daddy said when he climbed this tree, he understood things, and I thought . . ." Jessica gazed up into the murmurous fluttering leaves above her. "I was sure he'd be here," she said.

She looked at her mother's suffering face, and it seemed as if her father *were* somewhere nearby, smiling that little smile at Jessica, waiting for her to do the right thing. No, it wasn't Mom's fault, and it wasn't fair to blame her. It was nobody's fault. It had just happened. He had gone out in the rain for ice cream and it had just happened.

"Sometime when I'm not so tired, I'll carve your name on the tree with ours, Mom," Jessica said.

"Will you? Thanks, darling. I'd like that." Mom hugged Jessica. Then she began speaking in that eager voice she used when she knew how to fix something. "Would you like it if I explained what this tree means to us to the people who bought the house? They might let us come back whenever we like. I'm sure they would. They're lovely people."

Jessica didn't answer. Quickly, Mom continued, "If you want, we could bring Daddy's ashes here. It's true that he loved this tree. He might like being here better than being far away on some mountaintop." Tears slid down Mom's cheeks.

"Okay," Jessica said. She touched her mother's wet cheek lovingly. "Okay, let's do that. And I'll bring flowers. Daddy loved flowers, wild ones, even dandelions and daisies, but black-eyed Susans were his favorite."

"They're bright gold and strong like my daughter," he had said.

And now Jessica was crying too. Weeping, finally, with all the pent-up force of her love and loss, she clung to her mother.

"It's time to get back to Hammond," Mom said when their tears were spent. She picked up the limp backpack and took Jessica's hand.

"Want me to carry you?" Alan asked Tycho.

"I'm not a baby," Tycho said indignantly. He took off ahead of everybody, going toward the van.

133

Daddy, Jessica thought as they passed the pet cemetery and the tears welled up hotly again. "Daddy," she whispered as they got near the grandparents' house where they didn't live anymore. "Daddy."

She looked back at the climbing tree with longing. "Daddy, you come with us," she commanded. And she reached for him deep inside herself — in the one place where she knew he'd always be.

Author's Note

The seed idea for *Daddy's Climbing Tree* came to me from a fan letter. One of my sensitive young readers suggested that I write a story about a girl who returns to a house where she used to live and finds it empty and strange to her. I loved that image and played with it in my mind for months during walks and long car rides and before falling asleep.

Somehow the empty house spoke of a deeper loss than that of place. It kept reminding me of my son's death, which I thought I had already worked out in words on paper—a form of self-therapy I've always used—in the book *Ghost Brother*. I kept thinking about my grandchildren, who had their wonderfully strong, protective father taken from them when my granddaughter was five and my grandson was three. Although Jessica is not *just* like my granddaughter, they share some qualities with a few of my own thrown in, and little brother Tycho is loosely based on my grandson. Some of the brother-sister relationship I've observed between my grandchildren is there as well.

The father was a quick sketch of a tremendously sympathetic male nurse my husband had for a difficult hospital procedure. I'm sure that young man will live a long life and be available for his two children during theirs, but his healing powers were so striking that I had to borrow him for my story. The mother is a teacher I knew once. Somehow having real people in mind for my characters helps me to pattern them accurately. That is, it gives me a reference point from which I try to think and react, as they might rather than as I would in any situation.

As I did in writing *Ghost Brother,* I cried a lot during the many drafts of this book. I hope it is a healing rather than a hurting book. What I meant to say is that we humans can endure the most unbearable loss and still set forth to love again. We're made of fragile stuff, and that ability to resurrect ourselves is our saving grace.